D&D. DUNGEON ACADEMY

No Humans Allowed!

Written by
MADELEINE ROUX

Illustrated by
TIM PROBERT

HARPER
—An Imprint of HarperCollinsPublishers

DUNGEONS & DRAGONS®

Dungeons & Dragons: Dungeon Academy: No Humans Allowed!
Dungeons & Dragons, D&D, their respective logos,
and the dragon ampersand, are registered trademarks of
Wizards of the Coast LLC. © 2021 Wizards of the Coast.
All rights reserved.

Manufactured in Spain.

www.harpercollinschildrens.com

ISBN 978-0-06-303912-4

Book design by Elaine Lopez-Levine

22 23 24 25 26 LBC 7 6 5 4 3
❖
First Edition

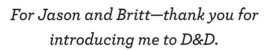

*For Jason and Britt—thank you for
introducing me to D&D.*

1

Zellidora "Zelli" Stormclash tapped her boot impatiently, watching the slaad's shiny eyelids click and clack as he blinked. Nobody was much pleased about the recent interdimensional exchange program that brought the slaadi to the school except the slaadi themselves, who seemed quite at home. Most of the students just wished they would take their slimy fingers and attitude back to their native realm, Limbo. But for the moment, Zelli took pity on this particular slaad. He was the smoothest frog kid in their grade, and that made him a target. No warts and no spines meant no intimidation, and that meant no respect. Nobody wanted to be the smoothest or prettiest kid at Dungeon Academy; they wanted to be the *scariest*.

Just a stone's throw from the dusty bookcase they huddled behind, a table of warty, spiny,

smelly (and therefore respected) slaadi hunched over a book, pointing and gurgling with laughter. Slaadi stuff. *Boy* stuff, probably. Zelli didn't know and she didn't particularly care.

"Which one of these dummies is giving you trouble?" she asked, stuffing the urge to fold her hands together and crack her knuckles. That would ruin the element of surprise. Slaadi were generally big, very big, and Zelli didn't relish the idea of tangling with one.

Gixi, the slumpy, trembling slaad at her side, pointed a circular fingertip toward the biggest frog of the bunch. "That one. He's the worst of the lot. The *worst*. He never leaves me a-alone, not for one second. When they relocated to Faerûn, his dad remarried a lesser drake and now he thinks he's king of the school. He says he—"

"Calm down, Gixi, I don't need his life story." She tapped the slaad on his moist shoulder and flapped her hand, waiting for him to show her the goods. Payment. She wasn't going to intervene on this tadpole's behalf for free. Generally, she stayed out of trouble. Generally. But this was a special occasion. "Show me the ring again."

The slaad pulled a tattered velvet box, about the size of a fist, out of the leather satchel slung around his shoulders. He pulled back the top and

revealed a large silver hoop, dented and flecked with . . . something. Mud, she hoped. *Please don't let that be adventurer blood.*

"It's all dinged up!" she sighed.

"Do you want it or not?"

"Fine, you sneak. Wait here."

Zelli pulled back her head and stormed out from around the bookcase, plunging into the little library alcove. Above the table where the slaadi had gathered, a wrought iron chandelier dripping wax and grease illuminated the goofball fest below. Rolling up her sleeves, she marched right up to the back of the big, warty slaad who Gixi had pointed out and tapped him on the shoulder.

"Look alive, slimeball."

The razor-backed frog boy swung around, a strangled sound of confusion glubbing out of him before Zelli reared back, drew in a huge breath, and roared right in his face.

Behind the bookcase, she heard Gixi burble with laughter as his rival and bully went end over end, toppling out of his chair with a croak of surprise. His friends erupted in peals of laughter, holding their mottled bellies and pointing, almost falling on the floor themselves.

"You should see your face!" a short green one shrieked.

"She got you so good!"

Zelli smiled and crossed her arms over her vest. "Leave Gixi alone or I'll be back to embarrass you again, and next time I'll do it in the dining chamber, got it?"

She didn't wait for a reply, the laughter going on and on as she returned to the gloating little slaad tucked safely behind the shelves. Before she could say a word, he thrust the velvet box into her hands, bouncing like the bubbling surface of an agitated slime. "Take it! Take it. You earned it, Zelli. You're the best!"

He made his escape before the other slaadi could realize he was there, leaving Zelli to stare down at the box with the banged-up ring and sigh. "I'm not the best," she murmured, making her own slow exit out of the school library. "I'm nobody."

Still, she had gotten the first thing she had come for. On her way out, she swung by the circulation desk. The Dungeon Academy Library soared up six levels, a dripping cavern filled with overflowing tomes, scrolls, manuals, and tablets, a maze of ladders and staircases that confused even the fifth-grade students. Zelli knew all the nooks and crannies, all the ins and outs. She spent plenty of time alone in that library, probably *too much*.

She could just hear her mother's growl of a

voice in her ear as she sauntered toward the circulation desk. *You need to make friends, Zelli. You need to try.*

Zelli loved her mother too much to point out that the reason nobody wanted to be her friend was also the same reason nobody messed with her much at school. The old winged, narrow-snouted kobold librarian, Shinka Bookbinder, stood behind the desk, reaching the edge of it by standing on four hefty tomes. She might have just used her wings to reach the desk, but she saved her energy for the times she needed to flap up to the highest recesses of the library to reach a book. Draped in musty linens, beads, and bits of scrolls tacked to her robe, the kobold peered over the top of her bent spectacles and smiled, handing Zelli the book she needed before she could ask for it. She immediately returned to her dusting, oh-so-lovingly handling a copy of *The Many Triumphs of the Waterdeep Dragons over the Dungeon Academy Flumphs*. It visibly sparkled, warded and charmed to protect against damage from the slimier students. To the right of Shinka Bookbinder was a mimic student worker who had transformed into a quill and dashed off late notices into an ink-splotched ledger.

"Thank you!" Zelli called, ring box in one hand and book in the other. She was lucky to nab the

one and only copy of that human adventurer manual, hoping to crank out an extra-credit essay for Professor Gast. Somehow, she was managing to fail History of Horrible Humans, and it was easier to just do the extra credit rather than unpack why that might be.

"Of course, my dear. Anything for Professor Stormclash's girl!"

The librarian had always had a soft spot for her, unlike every other professor at Dungeon Academy. Well, with one notable exception, and that was her next destination. Zelli dashed into the hall, casting a nervous glance at the giant swinging pendulum keeping time in the corridor. The pendulum itself was the old great ax of the Mad Smithy, a human barbarian who had tried (and mortally failed) to invade the school. The grand corridor ran the length of the central artery of the school, the ancient stone heart of the academy that housed the library, entrance, dining chamber, dean's quarters, and training arena.

Zelli raced down the corridor, a flurry of bats rustling overhead. She was mindful of the traps and triggers littering the ground, some lurking under threadbare carpets, others right out in the open. A hundred swinging blades and poisoned darts waited in recessed alcoves along the walls,

never used but there just the same, protection against any unwise adventurers tempted to breach the crumbling, craggy walls of Dungeon Academy and threaten its young students. The corridor smelled of damp and rot, wax and char, the elixir of the delve, of the dark and hidden places where monsters seethed in the dark. There were few monsters in the dark here, for they all conducted their business right out in the open, the future denizens, horde-keepers, trap-springers, and creepy-crawlies of the most treacherous dungeons in Faerûn.

Nobody waved at Zelli as she hurried east down the corridor and toward the training arena, and she didn't spot any of the usual snitching hall monitors. Jizek, a dao who liked to skulk up and down the hall in the shadows, was a particularly nasty suck-up, and she derived real delight in tattling on any student who wasn't where they were supposed to be. Dao, of course, could detect both good and evil intent, so Jizek was just as likely to report truancy as she was a student committing an abhorrent act of kindness. Lend a helping hand? Jizek told on you. Compliment a goblin on their sweater vest? Detention. Offer someone half of your snack? Jizek would know and turn a sharp eye, and punishment could swiftly follow. A wave of sound surged from the wide-open double wooden doors leading to the

dining chamber as she passed it. She glanced over her shoulder at the pendulum again—just enough time, she decided, to find her mother, then shovel some gruel into her mouth in the chamber while finishing her extra-credit essay before next period.

Her mother's voice came to her again, this time even more exasperated. *By all the Nether Scrolls in Netheril, Zellidora Stormclash, do your work on time!*

Zelli didn't need to imagine her mother's voice just then as she slipped out the East Dungeon door and into the biting cold of a wintry afternoon. Professor Kifin Stormclash thundered across the Goreball pitch, her steps reverberating off the mountain stones concealing the academy from the wider world, echoing far across the field and stopping every student dead in their tracks. The reason nobody at the academy befriended Zelli or bothered her was standing tall and proud in the long grass, her horns curved and sharp, her tail banded with steel rings, her height and sturdy build giving her more the appearance of a statue than of a living, breathing creature.

"Pathetic!" Professor Stormclash bellowed. "Will you trip and fall over your own feet when humans come to invade your borderlands?"

She was busy drilling a dozen or so gnoll

students in the year above Zelli. They were all flea-bitten and scarred, shaggy and brawny, fanged and maned and mean, except when faced with a minotaur professor. A wet dog funk hung around them as they cowered before Zelli's mother.

"Now prepare to spring upon your enemy again, and this time do not disappoint the demon lord Yeenoghu," Professor Stormclash was saying as Zelli approached. Her tattered boots whispered through the grass as she trotted up to the towering minotaur. A few of the gnolls sniggered at the sight of her, then thought better of it and settled down onto their haunches to practice their skulking. Zelli turned a harsh eye on them—drawing the ire of a minotaur was one thing; drawing the

ire of a minotaur mother was quite another.

"Honey!" Her mother noticed her and bent down to greet her. Zelli didn't know how they were fooling anyone—the fake horns on her head and tail pinned under her trousers didn't make her look anything like her adoptive minotaur mother. Then again, nobody had the courage to point that out to Professor Stormclash, who could pulverize them with one swing of her fist. Her tone turned sharp as she noticed the book tucked under Zelli's arm. "Doing our homework over lunch again, I see."

"It's just extra reading," she muttered, then thrust out the velvet box toward her mother. "Happy birthday."

"Oh, honey. You didn't need to get me anything." She glanced inside the box and smiled down at the nose ring, even though it was bent and dirty. "Zellidora, it's wonderful. You're such a ray of darkness. Thank you."

The minotaur bent lower, as if to plant a kiss on Zelli's profusion of springy black curls. Zelli ducked her head away and cleared her throat, eyes roaming pointedly to the gnolls peering at them from the tall grass.

"Very well, I won't embarrass you."

"Gotta go," Zelli chirped, turning before anyone could notice her cheeks changing to a darker shade. "Reading, right?"

"And do not forget to eat! You will never grow to terrifying heights if you do not eat!"

Zelli waved off her mother's concerns and backtracked across the pitch, plunging back into the drippy dank cool of the academy corridor, then taking a sharp left into the dining chamber. While Mavis, the towering fire elemental cook, scooped and scorched slop onto a counter along the eastern wall, the students sorted themselves into their respective cliques—the myconids, fungus folk (or "fart breaths," as the bullies liked to call them), had claimed a table, puffing and sporing away, a fine haze of pollen hanging above them like a sneezy cloud; the kobolds gathered around a long trestle table toward the back, cackling over dice and haunches of roast meat; the mimics had accumulated like a stack of miscellany near the door, appearing rather like an adolescent's tumbled and rumpled room, though some chose to snack on the vermin prepared for them in their natural form, a gelatinous mass with nerves and a nucleus at the ooey-gooey center; the gnolls not currently terrorized by her mother feasted on raw and bleeding steaks in the northwest corner, with the slaadi contingent chumming

around not far away, giving a rousing, chest-puffed rendition of the academy's song:

We dwell! We're swell! We claw and roar and smell! We bump (in the night), we thump (with a fright), the DUNGEON ACADEMY FLUMPHS . . .

On and on it went, monsters, creeps, and creatures of all sizes, colors, and creation gossiping at full volume while a single human-as-minotaur slinked into the hall, swiped a bowl of burnt, flavorless porridge from Mavis, and found a tiny, empty, insignificant spot to mind her own business and dash off that last-minute, grade-saving assignment.

And that was exactly what Zelli intended to do, tucking into her lunch and elbowing open the torn and well-loved copy of *The Human Manual for Monsters and Dwellers*. A spurt of dust rose from the parchment as Zelli flicked the pages quickly, landing on the chapter that corresponded best to their current textbook reading assignment. The moment she did, she felt the gruel in her stomach drop straight to her toes. A portrait in inks and watercolors headed the chapter, an image of a fierce human woman who might have been Zelli's twin. Beneath her, the caption read: *Allidora Steelstrike, the Unyielding Blade.*

All the air, sense, and blood ran out of her. The

woman, posed with a tremendous sword nearly half her height (Zelli herself favored swords), had been depicted with an explosion of black curls piled on her head, dark skin, and catlike yellow eyes that even simply in a drawing appeared to twinkle with mischief.

My Zelli, never not up to no good, Professor Stormclash liked to say. *Eyes full of secrets.*

Zelli wasn't foolish enough to think herself a real minotaur. She had, for a while, but not once she grew up enough to see the stark and obvious differences between her and the two minotaur matriarchs raising her. Kifin and Iasme were as close to her as could be, and were wonderful mothers who she trusted and cared for. But a wedge had

ALLIDORA STEELSTRIKE
THE UNYIELDING BLADE
Known adventurer and enemy to all
monsters and creatures of Faerûn.

dropped between them the night they sat her down and explained that she was not one of them, not a minotaur destined to haunt a deadly maze or hunt adventurers across a vast and unyielding desert, but that Iasme had found her while out foraging one day, a tiny *human* baby, pea-sized in their large eyes, helpless and frail, wailing in a basket behind a curtain of wavering reeds. A human baby. *Humans, the enemies of monsters everywhere.*

They hid her, of course, and dressed her up as a minotaur, and, with Kifin's respected position at the academy, had her enrolled. Nobody questioned one minotaur, let alone the will of two, and so life went quietly on for Zellidora Stormclash. Zelli had always wondered why her mothers hadn't been more afraid of taking in a human. Only once had she worked up the courage to ask, and Iasme had shrugged and said, "Your mother is not afraid of anything." But there was a look in the minotaur's eye that told Zelli there was more to it, and Iasme had looked so sad then that she decided not to pry.

"This is her," Zelli breathed, seeing herself reflected in the woman's eyes, her posture, her attitude. Her *name*. "This is my real mother."

And her real mother was the subject of her next class, History of Horrible Humans. She took a deep breath and tried to read, but her eyes had glazed with unexpected tears. No. Nobody could see that. Crying during lunch was not allowed at Dungeon Academy. Wiping at her face, Zelli forced herself to shut the book and try to eat. Her hand shook, and she just hoped she was as invisible in that moment as she had always been at school.

The spoon was halfway to her lips when, with a shriek, an owlbear roughly the size of an outhouse crashed through her table, sending her, the porridge, and *The Human Manual for Monsters and Dwellers* flying across the room.

2

Wearing her porridge, Zelli reached for the wooden sword strapped to her back, leaping to her feet as three owlbears trundled up to the table, looming over her and their horned, feathered brethren. She only hoped her horns weren't falling off her head, giving her away.

"You forgot this, Hugo." A brown, shaggy owlbear missing a good deal of his head feathers dropped a half-eaten turkey leg near them. "Pick it up and eat it."

Zelli recognized the leg dropper from her Tricksters and Traps class. He sat in the back and never raised his hand and mumbled out a wrong answer whenever called upon, then scoffed, like maybe learning things was the dumbest idea in the world. There was a mean glint to his red eyes that Zelli didn't appreciate.

"If you don't mind, I was trying to finish my reading," Zelli growled. She glanced at the big owlbear, Hugo, still cowering on the floor. The dining chamber had gone silent. Great. Attention, the last thing she wanted. She also wasn't keen on catching detention time for this—she had almost gotten in big trouble with Professor Cantrip the week before when she helped up a student in the hall who had tripped and scattered their homework. *No* kindness allowed at Dungeon Academy.

"Put the sword down; our quarrel is with him." Another owlbear joined to loom over them and sneer. "Owlbears hunt. They kill. They eat what they hunt and they're proud of it. They don't eat salad."

That last word came out like a curse. Zelli

raised a brow and her sword a little higher. "This is all over *salad*?"

"You wouldn't get it," the shaggy, bedraggled owlbear muttered. "This is who we are. It's what we do. Why even come to the academy if you're not going to behave like a real owlbear?"

"He looks real enough to me," Zelli replied. A few kobolds had wandered over to see what the fuss was all about. As soon as she raised her sword, the myconid table cleared off, leaving behind nothing but a cloud of green spores. "Leave him alone. Who cares if he wants to eat lettuce?"

"We care," the other owlbear grunted. "Pick up the meat, Hugo. And eat it."

It was true that Zelli had never seen an owlbear, especially one of Hugo's immense size, shiver in fear on the ground, using a "minotaur" as a shield, and she had never seen one dive headfirst into a bowl of greens, either, but it didn't seem like he deserved this treatment.

A few gnolls joined the circle forming around them, and then the slaadi noticed, too. . . . Zelli scrunched up her nose, realizing this was becoming a real scene. She glanced around for help, then remembered nobody would stick up for her or for someone like Hugo. They might not pick a fight with her, but they weren't above gawking at whatever was about to happen right in the middle of the dining chamber. A chant began, chasing around the room and growing louder.

Eat it, eat it, eat it!

Hugo made a soft, strangled sound out of his beak and covered his face with both feathered arms. Zelli had seen enough. She kicked the turkey drumstick hard enough to send it sailing into the pond in the corner, then she drew in a big, fortifying breath and let loose one of her minotaur roars.

The chanting died down; the owlbears froze and then scattered. Their audience broke up, too, but not before a few fingers and claws were pointed, a few whispers had, and a few laughs shared at their expense.

She had just defended a Big Loser in front of everyone. In front of half the academy. She hardly cared about the owlbear one way or the other, but other students cared, and they wouldn't forget. Zelli wiped a glob of porridge off the end of her nose and returned her sword to its sheath, then turned and offered Hugo her hand. *Well,* she thought, *I'm already in deep—in for a copper, in for a gold.*

"Are you all right?" she asked.

"Only wounded pride, I'm afraid." Hugo spoke with a gentle lilt, softer and sweeter than the other owlbears who had come to yell at him about his eating habits. They wandered back to her quiet end of the table. Zelli picked up her fallen book and used her sleeve to clean off the food splattered across the cover.

"Thank you," he said, shy. He was one of the largest owlbears at the academy, white and brown, with a silvery glint to the ends of his feathers. His curved beak was butter yellow, and his eyes sky blue. "I never

Thank
You...

expected to be saved from bullies by a bully."

Zelli frowned and hunched over her book. "I am *not* a bully."

Hugo blinked at her rapidly. "Nobody wants to be on the wrong end of your roar. Last semester you kept that goblin Dennis the Thorax from throwing a mimic off the third-story battlement. And last week you chased Fleshmelter off the Goreball pitch for that skinny kobold with one ear."

Maybe he had a point. "I only did that for the kobold because I wanted his new training sword, and it's not like Fleshmelter was going to use it. He's a gelatinous cube; he doesn't even have hands! That doesn't make me a bully."

"A bully of bullies, then." Hugo's eyes twinkled. "Something like a hero!"

She snorted and tried to fish a bit of porridge out of her bowl with a crooked finger. "I'm certainly no hero. I'm a nobody."

"Not at all. We are all beginning to take notice—you champion the small, the shy, the non-threatening," he explained.

Zelli groaned. That's just what she didn't need, to be known as Queen of the Losers. *Delightful.*

"And even if you think you're nobody, I am grateful all the same," he replied, inclining his

head with decidedly un-owlbear-like grace. He then reached over and swiped a porridge-covered mushroom from her shoulder with one claw.

"You like plants, huh?" she asked. The pendulum outside in the corridor clanged, beginning to signal the end of their free hour.

"Well, this is a fungus," Hugo replied, indicating the wilted mushroom. He chuckled, as if everyone knew that. "But indeed. I am quite fascinated by all things herbal, fungal, and floral. Plants are endlessly interesting, and also delicious. In fact, many habitats could be protected and thrive if we pledged to eat less meat—"

The final pendulum clang chased Zelli out of her seat, book under arm, with Hugo tagging along behind her. She shot a look at him over her shoulder as they filed out toward the spiral staircase leading down to the first dungeon level.

"You're nice and all, but I go it alone," she said. "Nobody, remember?"

Hugo appeared not to hear her, still committed to extolling the virtues of his plant-only diet.

"Why, my own herd decimated the Harte Glade, and the damage to the ecosystem was unimaginable! It became a dead place, uninhabitable, and all because we could not temper our greed for meat. The same occurred in Starwood Forest. It is practically an epidemic of devastation. And I am not even demanding much, just moderation. . . . There must be a different way."

"Like everyone eating salad?" she teased, cold rushing up to meet them as they joined the stream of students lining up for the stairs.

"Perhaps!" he chuckled. "Perhaps."

"You're one strange owlbear, Hugo," Zelli said, shaking her head.

"How kind! Thank you!"

The path down to the dungeons curved around and around, ominous sighs and whispers of unknown origin hissing up like evil steam from the sheer drop on their left. That pit went to impossible depths, and Zelli suspected that not even their illustrious dean knew what was lurking down there. The students crowded to the right, making the delve in pairs and trios, swapping stories and complaints.

"This is my third go-around with Hoard Management; there's just so much stupid *math*," the lanky gnoll girl ahead of them grumbled to her friend, sticking a wad of chewed gum into a wrapper and then flicking it into the forever pit.

"Intro to Skulking isn't so bad," her kobold

companion said with a shrug. "Professor Scream-shatter goes easy on us at least."

Zelli jumped, startled by Hugo the owlbear tugging on her linen sleeve. Tucked into one of the brazier alcoves to their right, a rotund little kobold with one jagged ear up and one down paced and shrieked at another student, a mimic, currently transformed to appear like a rather serious book. A book, she discovered, with a full mouth of jagged, gleaming teeth, and even shinier metal braces.

"None of our business," Zelli whispered, urging Hugo down the next stair.

"But we might intervene!" Hugo stopped short, the students behind them forced to go around the big feathered roadblock. "Just as you intervened for me. Look at that poor dusty book; it needs our help."

"This is how you get into trouble," Zelli told him, but it *did* look unfair. Unjust. The kobold, even if it wasn't the scariest creature around, stood a head taller than the mimic, jabbing a finger into its face, which at that moment was two decorative paisley swirls and a horizontal slice in the book's leather cover.

Before Zelli could pull Hugo down the stairs, the kobold noticed them hovering and glared in their direction. She was familiar with him from class but had never bothered to learn his name. He seemed to size up Zelli, perhaps recognizing her, and jabbed a tiny clawed finger in her direction. "Tell thisss useless hunk of junk to do what it is meant to do and change formsss!" Missing a number of juvenile teeth, the kobold spat in a hundred directions as he talked, his voice like the scrape of a whetstone across steel. He whirled back to face the trembling mimic book and pointed at them instead. "Do it! Transssform! Anger me not! For my cousin is—a dragon!"

Zelli couldn't help but roll her eyes—that lizard pup couldn't possibly be related to a dragon. Not in  a million years would a drake be caught with a sniveling kobold, but the lie was so outrageous she almost respected it. That kind of audacious delusional thinking might actually take the little kobold far at Dungeon Academy, for growing up to challenge adventurers and heroic humans took courage, and he might at least have that.

"I c-can't do that," the mimic wailed, pages ruffling. "Shields are for fighting, and fighting is d-d-dangerous!"

Right before their eyes, the mimic shrank down into a small box with a lid and enameled handles, a miniature dancer turning behind a glass pane, gentle, tinkling music drifting out into the icy cold dungeon. Then it transformed again, this time into a quill; then it returned to its initial book form and whimpered.

"See? Nice things only. Nothing dangerous."

"Leave the paperweight alone, kobold," Zelli warned, gesturing for Hugo to follow her. "Come on, we're going to be late for Horrible Humans."

As if to remind them of just that, the pendulum in the corridor above clanged twice, the sound reverberating down around

them, loud enough to make Zelli's ears ring.

"I'm not a paperweight! Just because I was voted *Least Likely to Change* in the yearbook doesn't mean I'm useless!" the mimic insisted, sliding forward with strange, smooth momentum. There were no legs attached to the book, but the mimic had no problem jetting around, almost like the slime students. "I'm Bauble! This is Snabla; he's my friend when he's not being a horrible meanie."

"Horrible! Meanie!" the kobold Snabla shrieked, sticking out his forked tongue at them all. A rickety wooden shield was strapped to his back, hardly more than refuse, a few old boards nailed together and mended hundreds of times. He had (badly) painted the wood and nails to look like dragon scales. "My cousin—"

"If your cousin is a dragon, then *my* cousin is the Lord Protector," Zelli teased.

"Hmph!" They all rushed downward, driven to haste by the pendulum's insistent clanging, the temperature growing colder by the step. "I only

wanted to know what it felt like to hoissst a mighty shield! A true kobold of worth mussst carry the kind seen upon the likes of my father, the Great Wyrm Sneef the Unending. Hisss was a shield of fine dragon leather, and with it, he hoarded mountainsss of gold, gold even to rival the hordes of dragonsss!"

First the dragon cousin and now Sneef the Unending. Zelli was beginning to think this kobold really was imagining things. The book tucked under her arm seemed to grow heavier. Then again, she had just discovered that her own mother might be Allidora Steelstrike, the sodding Unyielding Blade and topic of their next class. This secret to her origin had been there all along, and only unearthed now thanks to a stupid assignment. She pinched the bridge of her nose, suddenly aware that Hugo and the scuffle with the owlbears, and now this business with Snabla and Bauble, had all just been a momentary distraction. She didn't want to think about the fact that she could be the long-lost daughter of an epic human hero.

While she grew more and more nervous with each descended stair, Hugo gently raised a question to Snabla, his voice ever kind and solicitous. "Why did you not inherit your father's fine shield, Snabla?"

"I'm not worthy," the kobold lamented, throwing his wiry arms into the air. "My father thinksss me a coward."

"You are," Bauble sniffed. "You wanted me to turn into that mighty shield for you. How would that ever prove your worthiness to anyone? I've actually done quite a bit of reading on kobold culture, and cheating your way to that shield would bring far more dishonor than just never inheriting it in the first place. In fact—"

"Don't go proving your worthiness," Zelli warned them all, interrupting the mimic's lecture. They at least reached the darkened, dripping gloom of the first dungeon level. Puddles and cracks abounded, and behind those cracks, peeks at perilous lava pools far below. "Me? I'm going to fail whatever I have to, over and over again, so they don't send me off to the dungeons."

"That makesss two cowardsss," Snabla cut in, racing to catch up to Zelli and walk beside her.

They stopped outside the second massive door on the left, shuffling into the mass of students who had gathered for History of Horrible Humans. While they waited, Hugo tucked a few claws under his chin and made a soft, thoughtful sound.

"There is some merit to what you say, Zelli," he told them. Bauble's paisley-swirl eyes blinked

in confusion. "For the students sent to terrorize Horntree Village have not returned, and they are the oldest and most terrifying among us. Patty was just named valedictorian, and Gutrash is the captain of the Goreball team. If *they* could fail . . ."

"They'll return," Bauble murmured, pages trembling once more. "Won't they?"

Zelli shrugged, and both Snabla and Bauble gulped. An image flashed before her eyes, of Allidora Steelstrike charging toward the diminutive kobold and the flustered book, sword flashing, teeth gnashing, a snarl tearing out of her throat before the Unyielding Blade chopped them in two.

Class was about to begin, but Zelli hesitated at the door. She watched Hugo, Snabla, and Bauble go forward. Chilled, she forced herself to follow. "They aren't teaching us to hold hands and sing 'tra-la-la' with adventurers," she reminded them. Again, the book beneath her arm felt weighty. Impossibly heavy. "Once you leave this mountain, you're on your own in the dungeons, and the dungeons are where heroes go to hunt."

3

A magicked stick of chalk squeaked across the board, outlining that day's subject—the family tree of Allidora Steelstrike, known adventurer and enemy to all monsters.

Their demilich instructor, Professor Gast, was merely a floating bespectacled skull engulfed in blue flames, hovering back and forth in front of the filling chalkboard. Gast was hated by just about every student at the academy, and, Zelli suspected, by most of the staff, too. Undead weren't welcome, not even among monsters, but he had once been a well-respected and feared hobgoblin wizard. The story went that he had journeyed toward Waterdeep to lecture on the perils of adventurers and on the way, ironically, died from a human ambush. When he turned up again on school grounds, nothing but a bewitched hobgoblin head, nobody

could convince him he was dead or different. Professor Gast now fastidiously avoided mirrors. His lack of body did not mean lack of knowledge, and he had a habit of droning on and on and on, making History of Horrible Humans class *the* prime nap hour.

But not this time.

This time, she sat listening closely, absorbing every petrifying fact about what she was becoming more and more convinced was her extended family. Hugo, Snabla, and Bauble had all chosen desks in her vicinity, but Gast's lecture was distracting enough to keep her from worrying about them clinging to her like monster barnacles.

"The Steelstrike legacy is one that should strike fear into the heart of any wise dungeon dweller," Gast wheezed, bobbing back and forth, the magicked chalk underlining the word *DANGER* three times on the blackboard behind him. He had a voice like the steam whistling off a kettle. "Marked by their signature battle cry, one will always be warned when a Steelstrike has entered the dungeon."

Zelli's eyes widened. Battle cry? Like a battle *roar*? All this time, she had assumed her roaring acumen came from the lessons her own minotaur mother had given, but maybe this was something

passed down in the blood. And there she had gone all around the school, roaring her tail off, giving herself away. She glanced around at her fellow students, but only Hugo regarded her back. His eyes, by contrast, narrowed. Was he noticing the painfully obvious resemblance between her and the woman illustrated in the manual she had procured from the library? She had only been paying attention to the owlbear for a brief time, but already she could tell he was sharper than most. He kept his head down in class, and she couldn't remember him ever raising his paw to answer a question, but maybe he just wanted to avoid attention from the other owlbears.

Fumbling, Zelli reached up to make sure her fake horns were still on straight.

"Those few who have survived encounters with the Steelstrike family suggest that they are susceptible to spring traps, for while they are a hardy bunch, they are not particularly nimble. . . ."

Zelli grimaced at that. So she wasn't the most graceful person in the world; that didn't make her clumsy enough to fall for a spring trap! *Don't take it personally; you don't want to be related to these humans, remember?*

"But while they may have the occasional weakness, a monster must never underestimate a Steelstrike," Gast continued. A scream from outside the classroom interrupted, but it was a distant and echoing one, and so commonplace as to not be noticed. Loud enough to shake the manacles and cages hanging from the walls of the classroom, it only gave Professor Gast the slightest of pauses. "Theirs is a lineage of strength, perseverance, and dogged pursuit of dungeonly riches. They have never met a challenge they cannot conquer, proudly wearing the scars of numerous battles, considered by their wretched human peers to be

ennobled, kindly, and the bravest heroes."

Ennobled? Kindly? Zelli's face flamed hot and red. Her hands balled up into fists on the desk. These dratted humans had abandoned her in a basket with nothing but a blanket and a scrap of leather with the name Zellidora carved into it. Kindly! Brave! Now she was going to grow up among monsters and, as all monsters did, get sent out into the dungeons to be slaughtered by delving heroes. They had consigned her to a cruel fate, to be an outsider all her life, and then to die in a far-off, dingy dungeon, just another half-remembered foe.

"Lies! They're not brave at all!" She heard herself shout it and found herself suddenly on her feet with enough force to knock her desk to the side. One of her horns fell somewhat askew, and she scrambled to fix it. The whole class, including Professor Gast, went dead quiet. All eyes were on her as she breathed heavily, realizing that she hadn't just imagined interrupting, but had actually done it.

"I beg your pardon, Miss Stormclash? Did you

have something to relate to the class?" Professor Gast paused, as did the chalk behind him. "I should expect a student of your years to know that it is classroom etiquette to raise one's hand before an outburst."

A few students giggled at that. Zelli pinched her lips together tightly, her anger only swelling at their laughter. "It's not an outburst, it's the truth! These humans are cowards, they're ... Who would be afraid of a defenseless baby?"

"A defenseless ..." An invisible force adjusted the professor's spectacles, which had begun to slide down. "Please be seated, Miss Stormclash; I have not finished today's lesson."

"I won't sit down! I refuse to learn about these humans! I hate them!" She was already in trouble, she reasoned, and so she collected her things and turned on her heel, living up to her adoptive mother's name and storming out of the class.

"Miss Stormclash!" she heard Gast calling frantically after her. "Unacceptable, young lady! That is detention! Report to the dean's office!"

Zelli would do more than that, she thought, much more. She would return to the dormitories, pack up her things, and leave the academy for good. Her heart clenched at the thought of leaving her mothers, but they would just have to

understand. She would leave them a note, explain everything—she didn't belong at the school, or among monsters; she didn't really belong anywhere.

She trekked back up to the main corridor, avoiding the familiar traps, running and running, avoiding, she knew, the hounds of hard truths nipping at her feet. *Where could she go?* she wondered. *Who would want her?* Not the Steelstrikes, certainly, not after she had been raised by minotaurs since infancy and then trained for the rest of her life by gelatinous cubes and beholders and giants coaching PE. How long until someone realized she wasn't actually a minotaur? And if nobody ever discovered her secret, how long until they stuck her in a maze somewhere, not as strong or sizable or unstoppable as a real minotaur, doomed to a lonely watch until some human came to destroy her?

The dean's office, sitting behind a massive, embellished door flanked by two sphinx statues, appeared on her left. Zelli hastened her stride, ready to fly right on by, not at all prepared to hear the booming voice of Dean Zxaticus through the open door.

"They will return," he was saying emphatically. "We must give them time."

Zelli skidded to a stop on her boots a few feet past the door, then backtracked to kneel down and listen. She risked peering around one of the sphinx heads, finding the imposing, many-tentacled, many-spectacled Zxaticus hovering above a rune-etched carpet, Professor Cantrip—an alchemist caught in an oozing emerald cube—pacing a wet streak back and forth across that same carpet. Zelli had always thought a gelatinous cube was a mindless, sticky blob just waiting to digest adventurers, but somehow Cantrip had managed to stay alive and develop some kind of symbiotic relationship with the oozy substance slorping him across the floor. Impro Vice, the mimic alchemy professor, was also present in their natural blobular form.

"What if they encountered too many obstacles?" Professor Cantrip asked, his voice muffled through the gelatinous goo trapping him upside down. "Horntree Village is but ten miles north of here; they should have returned yesterday at the latest."

"I concur," Impro Vice added. "This is most concerning. Gutrash is a formidable leader, but still so young."

Dean Zxaticus blinked his main immense, veiny, purple eye and all the others attached to

his tentacles turned away from them, and he hovered, if at all possible, with detectable hesitation. A few of his tentacles had their own single lenses, the eyes attached to them owlishly huge from the magnification. "There are . . . rumors of a most unnerving nature. Whispers of *adventurers* entering the region."

The two professors gasped in unison. Out in the hallway hidden behind the sphinx, Zelli did, too. Something deep inside, a trustworthy but annoying voice, bubbled up to tell her she knew what was coming next. Her stomach went tight. She clutched the statue with enough force to crack

the stone, palms wet with nervous sweat, her heartbeat quickening as the dean growled out the most sinister thing she could imagine.

"One sighting should make us all tremble," he said. "That of Allidora Steelstrike, the Unyielding Blade. Bane protect them, for if they happened upon that human, they are already lost."

Huh?!

4

Allidora Steelstrike. Zelli pushed away from the sphinx statue, standing, her mouth hardening into a firm line of resolve. It was time to get answers. *Why had the Steelstrikes abandoned her? Why didn't they want her? What would they say if they knew she was now living a double life as the very thing they hated and hunted?* If she left and left soon, she could find answers, and avoid any problems with students or staff—her outburst in class had nearly knocked her horns clean off. Surely someone had noticed; surely someone would start asking questions.

She was a human; she didn't want to know what happened when anyone on school grounds started asking the right questions. Her mothers were powerful and intimidating, but they couldn't protect her from every single creature

at Dungeon Academy.

"So, when do we leave?"

She stood, whirled, and clapped her hands over her mouth before a shriek could escape. Hugo, Snabla, and Bauble were there watching her, eavesdropping on the same conversation only a few yards away.

"How long have you been standing there?" she asked, crossing her arms over her chest.

"Long enough to know our classmates are in trouble," Bauble said. Still transformed into a large book, the mimic paced in a circle. "We didn't mean to surprise you!"

"Yesss, we did," Snabla spat. "Hugo isss head of the Lurking Club."

That explained how an owlbear of his size could sneak up on her. He did have the stink of an overachiever. The other two were small enough to not make much noise, and after all, she had been rather distracted by the prospect of being reunited with her long-lost human family. Right. That. She sighed and shook her head, then pushed past them, marching down the corridor toward the western fork, which would take her to the lift that offered access to the dormitories.

"You shouldn't go alone!" Hugo called, hurrying after her. The slide of pages across the floor

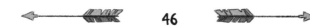

and the pitter-patter of little feet told her the others were giving chase, too.

"Who says I'm going anywhere?" Zelli refused to look at them.

"You stand up for the endangered," the owlbear pointed out when he was at her side. His big legs made catching her easy.

"You don't know anything about me." And that was true. Hugo couldn't know her real motives for leaving, or what she hoped to discover once she reached Horntree Village.

"Ssshe wants all the glory for herself!" Snabla cried. "But I will go; my shield is ready!"

He banged heartily on the shield face, a few wooden scales snapping and falling off. Snabla hurriedly scooped them away with his toes, turning a funny color.

They had nearly reached the lift, the massive, clattering chains as thick as tree trunks in sight. Zelli knew then that she couldn't outrun them, and that they were annoyingly persistent, so as soon as they reached the landing outside the platform, she spun and gave them each a deliberately cross look. She would roar only if they forced her hand.

"Your 'shield' is nothing more than a few busted toothpicks," Zelli told the kobold, pointing at his rickety prized possession. His torn ears

lowered, even more bedraggled as she yelled at him. They wouldn't last a second outside the school, and they wouldn't last a blink against Allidora Steelstrike, her potential family. "And you can't turn into anything useful at all." She leveled this at the mimic, who instantly poofed into a decorative pillow and hid behind Snabla. "And you're a vegetarian! A vegetarian owlbear! Who needs that? Who needs any of you? You're not ready for adventures or danger; you're better off staying here, safe and sound behind the dungeon walls."

Zelli stepped onto the lift and pulled the lever, and kept her back to them. This was for their own good, so why did she feel oily all over, like she badly needed a bath? She closed her eyes tight and listened to the gears rattling as she rose higher and higher, leaving three hurt monsters on the landing below.

You can't go where I'm planning to go, she thought, resolute once more. She just had to get through detention, then she would be gone. *If you knew what I really was, if you knew I was a human, you wouldn't want to follow me. You'd want me dead.*

Skipping detention was a surefire way to get noticed, and at that moment, Zelli wanted anything but.

So she went, dreading it with every tense muscle and sinew in her body. It took her a while to find the detention hall. Surprisingly, this was her first time, most of her scuffles with bullies swept under the rug and forgotten; they walked away with their pride bruised, and no big tough gnolls or prideful bugbears wanted to admit they had been beaten by the skinniest minotaur on the planet. Since it was nothing but silent time to contemplate her wrongdoing, Zelli decided to use it to consider even more wrongdoing, the kind that wouldn't just get her detention but suspension.

But she had to go. Even detention was a risk. Everyone turned to stare at her as she finally arrived at the hall, four minutes late. She shrank, hoping that her horns were perfectly straight and

believable as she kept her head down and crossed the ominously swaying, perilously narrow bridge that led to the suspended stone platform of the detention hall. Below, probably leaking over from the flowing lava lake beneath the dungeons, lay a bubbling magma pool. Her clothes itched, her skin already prickling with sweat, though the roiling red lava lay far, far below.

It was Professor Viletongue's turn to preside over the hall, her thin, withered body curled over a granite podium at the opposite edge of the platform from where Zelli had arrived. Her brittle hair trailed down to her waist, a backpack's worth of pencils and erasers caught in the scraggly mane. Professor Viletongue either didn't notice them there or didn't care. A night hag—Zelli couldn't imagine a more perfect creature to watch over detention. A hag's most coveted prize was virtue turned to villainy. And even a brief stay in this place could turn the Goodiest Two-shoes into a miscreant fit for the academy. The magma below churned, bubbling like a cauldron. Zelli noticed familiar faces staring at her as she shuffled onto the platform and hunted for an empty desk—Hugo, Snabla, and Bauble had all managed to land themselves in detention, too. It was too stupid to be a coincidence.

"What are you doing here?" she muttered out

of the corner of her mouth as she passed them.

Bauble the book bounced giddily on their desk. "I pretended to be a cabinet for Goreball uniforms and scared the cocaptain so badly I think she soiled herself. I've always wanted to see the Hall of Eternal Suffering and Monotony. Isn't it incredible? It's so . . . so . . . hot! They say a dozen students have perished here from sheer boredom."

Snabla appeared less thrilled, and actively avoided making eye contact with Zelli. That was just fine with her; she had hoped her speech to them in the hallway had frightened them off for good. "I told Gast he's just a dummy dumb sssskull," the kobold sighed. "He no believe. Snabla sssent here anyway."

And the unlikeliest denizen of the Hall of Eternal Suffering and Monotony detention hall went last. Hugo clacked his talons together nervously, crammed into the desk like a giant stuffed into a lunch sack.

"I—ahem—did nothing."

Zelli snorted and shook her head. Even whispering, they had drawn the roving eye of Professor Viletongue, who squinted in their direction.

"I just came along," Hugo added glumly. "Apparently they will not actually stop you from coming here voluntarily." He glanced around and

shivered. "And who would?"

"Good question." Zelli kept moving, taking a desk a few rows ahead of the others. A gnoll with a heavy patchwork of scars and a crooked snout growled at her from the right-hand corner. Two stoop-shouldered ogres passed notes to her left. Zelli slumped down into a desk and found that someone had carved there a rudimentary portrait of Cindro the Youngling, last year's Waterdeep Dragons' prom king.

"Pathetic," she muttered, covering the idiotic portrait with her

Gulp!

elbow. Professor Viletongue cleared her throat, her eyes becoming somehow even squintier as she glared at Zelli. She appeared to consult a long, long, curling roll of parchment on her desk, a scroll no doubt with the list of detention attendees and their crimes.

"Tsk, tsk, tsk," she heard the old night hag spit from her podium.

The platform fell silent then, save for the constant bubbling of the lava below. The fake horns on Zelli's head were killing her, the bases poking into her skin, the heat making her scalp sweat unbearably. She fidgeted and closed her eyes, then

Don't Look Down!

crossed her arms and laid her chin on her fore-arms. Maybe she would be the thirteenth student to die of boredom. And anxiety. Her leg bounced. She wanted to be gone, to be out of the academy and on her way to Horntree Village before anyone realized her plans or discovered her real identity.

Behind her, she gradually noticed whispers. She glanced over her shoulder to find Hugo, Sna-bla, and Bauble all leaning close to one another, discussing something urgently. As soon as she did, they shut up. Zelli slowly turned around, then whipped back to catch them mid-whisper. The owlbear scratched "innocently" at his neck.

"What are you planning back there?" she mur-mured, risking Viletongue's wrath. The massively thick chains holding the platform suspended above the lava shifted, and the whole floor swayed.

"Nothing!" said Bauble, while Snabla stuck out his tongue with a spitty "Sssecrets!"

Hugo nudged the kobold gently.

"Right." Zelli rolled her eyes. "Nothing secrets."

"None of your businessss!" Snabla said, with real venom.

"Be kind," Hugo warned, in a far gentler tone. "Though it is hard to do while our classmates are in danger...."

"Hugo is right, this is serious," Bauble chided,

though it sounded as if they were saying it to Zelli, too.

"Only because you have ssstinky crush on Gutrash!" Snabla snapped at the mimic, batting his eyes.

"Do not!" the mimic cried.

"Do too!"

The platform lurched suddenly, making everyone except the professor gasp. A wail, seemingly from nowhere, pierced the echoing nothingness around them, a shuddering, screaming cry silencing all of them. Hugo looked ready to molt.

"What was that?" he whispered, shaking.

"You're being too loud," Zelli replied, pressing one finger to her lips. "So be quiet."

And stop scheming. Whatever you're planning, just stop.

It took only a minute or so for the whispers to start up again, this time more audible.

"Do not," came Bauble's squeak.

"You do! You do, you do! You want ssstinky goblin Gutrash to take you to the spring dance! Prance and prance with Gutrash!"

"This is not what we came here to discuss," Hugo interrupted them, and that was enough to usher in another shimmy from the platform and a long, keening wail from whatever upset spirit

haunted the hall. Whoever had devised this place for detention had really known what they were doing.

"Come sit with us," Hugo encouraged her, gesturing.

She sighed. "No. Leave me alone."

"Come on," he said. "The desk beside me is free."

"*No.*"

Zelli rearranged her arms, revealing again the scratched portrait of Cindro the Youngling. Nobody would shut up about their rivalry with the Waterdeep Dragons, but Zelli couldn't care less. Of course they were better at everything: their scales were hard as steel, they could fly, and they could breathe fire. How could a bunch of gangly adolescent kobolds compete with that? Some people just didn't know their place, she thought, then winced. *Like me. Do I know my place? Is it here? Is it out there?*

There were no windows in the Hall of Eternal Suffering and Monotony, but Zelli found herself staring at where one might logically be. Her leg twitched again. She looked at the professor, at the gnolls, at the students behind her conspicuously trying to be inconspicuous, an owlbear, a mimic, and a kobold. This was ridiculous. Who

was she kidding, trying to fit in here? She didn't belong, that much was certain. Maybe she didn't belong with the humans, either, and maybe her two mothers really did think she could hack it as a minotaur one day, but whatever her fate was, it seemed certain she had to find it for herself.

Steelstrike or Stormclash . . . what am I?

She laid her head down on her arms again and tried to shut out the whispers.

What am I? she asked again, trying to just close her eyes and sleep. *Whatever it is, I won't find out in here.*

Zelli wasn't exactly head of the Lurking Club like Hugo, but she had paid attention well enough in Advanced Sneakcraft & Skulkery and knew that waiting for nightfall was wisest. And so she did, listless after detention until sunset, stuffing a pack with rope, dried fruit, flint, a few coins from her allowance, and a fresh linen shirt and doublet. Other than her textbooks, her entire life, it seemed, fit in one traveler's bag. Even during semester breaks, Zelli lived on school grounds, since her professor mother had permanent housing at the academy.

This place is all I know.

As she quietly packed her things (her ooze

roommate Bloppy sleeping deeply across the way), Zelli tore a piece of parchment from her school notes and found a quill on her desk, still ready from that morning's homework. How to start? How to ... Zelli wiped her sleeve across her eyes blindly, knowing the tears would come soon. She squinted down at the uneven, wrinkled parchment, writing by moonlight, the window already cranked open and the rope dangling there. Waiting for her. She didn't dare light a candle and wake Bloppy, the quiet, bookish ooze slumbering beneath a Dungeon Academy Flumphs pennant.

Moms, Zelli wrote, the quill scratching loudly in the dead silence of the darkened room.

Moms—
I love you, I'll be back
soon. Please don't
worry about me.
—Z

She placed the note on her desk, beside the velvet box much like the one she had gifted her mother that morning for her birthday. Inside lay a filigree nose ring, one sized for Zelli's far smaller face. One day, when she was old enough, she would get to have her nose pierced. That was the minotaur way. But that was earned, and now she was running away from the earning.

I'm sorry I'm not what you thought I would grow up to be, she thought.

Zelli touched the box gently, then hoisted her pack onto her shoulders, clasped an old cloak around her neck, and tiptoed to the window. A sky crowded with stars lay draped across the landscape, everything outside the confines of the hidden mountain school still and almost peaceful, the trees down in the courtyard turned into what looked like tiny toys by the distance. She gulped, gripped the rope tightly, and swung out into the cold night air, shivering as she thought of the deathly sheer drop visible below her boots.

For a moment, the warm safety of her little shared room seemed tempting indeed. If she climbed back inside, she could crumple up the note and just get on with life, all of this recklessness forgotten. *No,* she breathed out, watching silvery curlicues float up and away. No, she would never

be able to forget what she had seen in that textbook or what she had heard in the dean's office. Inside that room, regret and frustration waited for her. Outside? Outside, there were answers.

Answers and danger.

Zelli went down the rope, not sure but sure enough. The way down was hard, and while she was strong for her age, Zelli had not anticipated how much weight the pack would add; almost at once her shoulders began to ache and her hands grew slick with sweat around the rope. The mountainous facade gradually sloped outward as she descended, giving her more divots and crags to dig her boots into, but even so, she could feel her hands beginning to slip. The fibrous rope cut into her palms, and the pain in her shoulders began to bother her in earnest.

Don't look down,
don't look down . . .

One boot slid right off the next foothold, a cascade of pebbles skittering down the rock, frightening her. She gasped and clung tighter to the rope, but it was no use—her hands were too

Gulp

snap

tired, her balance overturned from the sudden momentum of her foot falling out from under her. Just about level with the treetops, she did not have much farther to go.

Just hold on, just a little bit longer!

Zelli scrambled and scrambled, hands desperately scratching at the rope and then the sheer rock face of the mountain, but there was nothing to hold on to and Zelli cried out, tumbling free, plunging through the trees and down the mountainside.

5

With a cry and a thump, Zelli landed on something warm, squishy, and very much alive.

"Hugo!"

The owlbear groaned, flat on his stomach from the unexpected impact of a falling girl. She rolled off him quickly, dusting off her cloak, making certain she hadn't broken anything important on the way down. She had ripped her sleeve a bit, the only casualty in what could have been a terrible landing.

"We simply must stop meeting like this," Hugo muttered, climbing to his feet and unrumpling his fur and feathers.

They stood in a small clearing, a hollow where the tall and gnarled

trees grew in a crescent, a glugging and bubbling blood fountain warding off trespassers, a gargoyle spewing the red froth from its mouth, wings wide and arms raised to the sky. Zelli then noticed that she and Hugo were not alone; Snabla and Bauble were there, too, the mimic in a big leather satchel of Hugo's that he had leaned against the fountain base. The eyelike designs on Bauble's cover blinked up at Zelli, and Snabla hissed and brandished his shield, then realized it was her and tucked the thing back on his shoulder.

A makeshift rope of bedsheets lay curled beside Hugo's pack.

"What are you doing here?" she whispered, retreating to the wall and tugging twice on the rope with deliberate jerks, undoing the slipknot high, high above in her room.

"Our classmates need us," Hugo pointed out calmly, though from the alert position of his ear feathers, Zelli could tell he was nervous. That wasn't surprising; none of them were allowed out of the school after dark without special permission from the dean's office. "We made our plans during detention. I tried to invite you!"

"We will find them," Snabla added, apparently fearless as he struck a heroic pose. "And I will

prove myself worthy in my father's eyesss."

"You'll get yourselves killed is what you'll do!"

"We won't let you go alone," Bauble added, finding their way out of the satchel and sliding toward her.

Zelli deflated, curling up the rope with slumped shoulders. She couldn't believe they were still willing to go with her, to *help* her. "Even after everything I said to you?"

"We know you didn't mean it," said Bauble. "You were just trying to scare us off. But we're not scared. R-Right?" They looked to Hugo and Snabla for reinforcement.

"Right!" Snabla agreed, still striking his ridiculous pose.

Bauble went still and then transformed into an ornate lantern, which Snabla grinned at, then reached down and took by the handle, raising Bauble to light them all. Two round hooks on either side of the front pane blinked at Zelli. "You help other kids, so now we help you."

"I really can't persuade you to stay here?" Zelli asked, tucking the rope into her traveler's bag and pushing by them, into the thick slog of trees

surrounding the school grounds.

"I am afraid we are all rather determined," Hugo replied, both of them watching as Snabla raced on ahead, Bauble crying out for the kobold to slow down as the lantern light bounced along the forest floor, poor Bauble's hinges creaking and squeaking as they went.

"Strange," Zelli said quietly, following the trail of light through the trees, touching each rough-barked trunk as they walked farther and farther away from the mountain. The academy was concealed within a nondescript peak, one not challenging or foreboding enough to tempt curious adventurers. It looked like any other mountain in the region, though once one reached the forest surrounding it, the trees were nearly impenetrable, a confusing maze of identical cramped oaks. A few wards like the fountain were dotted around the campus grounds, warnings against the odd lost traveler. "It looks so ordinary from here," Zelli remarked, glancing back at the school just as the canopy of leaves above nearly blotted out the view of it entirely.

"And safe," Hugo sighed.

Maybe for you.

"You're going to be in a lot of trouble when you go back to the Academy, you know," Zelli

told him, sidestepping tumbled branches and logs as they veered north.

"But not you?" Hugo asked softly.

She gazed up at him, narrowing her eyes.

"Because you won't be going back," he stated. "Because you're not one of us. Because you're a human."

Zelli stopped, nearly tripping over a particularly crafty branch. "No, I'm . . . I mean. But you . . . How did you know?"

Hugo chuckled, the feathers around his neck puffing up in amusement. She hurried to catch up with him. "For one? I saw one of your horns go funny when you stormed out of Horrible Humans this afternoon. For another, you do not have hooves or fur, and it's quite obvious really, but most people don't really look at anything. They don't see what's past the tip of their beak."

Maybe she had underestimated Hugo. Zelli hitched her pack higher and blew out a long, tortured breath. "Then you know who I'm looking for. Why I'm really going. . . ."

"The resemblance is uncanny," Hugo admitted. It was a relief that she didn't have to say it aloud. "But that does not mean you belong with humans and not us. You weren't raised like other humans; you don't behave like they do or think like they do. You have a place at the academy, too. With us."

Zelli shook her head, noticing that the lantern light ahead was growing closer and brighter; Snabla and Bauble must have finally stopped.

"I don't know, Hugo," she murmured. "I don't know. Please, just . . . Just don't tell the others, not yet. I don't want them to know."

Hugo shrugged his immense furry shoulders. "If you wish. It is not my secret to tell."

"Doom! Disassster!" Snabla gasped and puffed as he came careening back through the trees, shoving Bauble into Hugo's hands as he bent double and clutched his knobby little knees, desperate for air.

"So soon?" Hugo asked, kneeling to examine the kobold. "What doom? What disaster?"

"Snabla ssstarves! A rumbling and grumbling mossst foul!" Snabla wailed, no longer clutching his knees but his stomach. "Food, you foolsss! I require food!"

"What did you pack?" Zelli asked, astounded that the kobold couldn't last ten minutes outside the academy walls without incident. "I have a bit of dried fruit and some hardtack. . . ."

"No! No! It will not do! It will not do!"

"We . . . Hmm." Hugo unearthed a canteen from his satchel, then peered down into it. When he shook it, it didn't make a sound. "It appears we have set out upon this adventure somewhat underprepared."

"*Somewhat?!*" Zelli tossed up her hands. She certainly did not have enough food to feed *all* of them. "Not a crumb of food among you? What were you doing that whole time in detention?"

"Not to worry, my fine famished friends," replied Hugo with a quavering smile. He swapped the canteen for a map, unfurling it with a flourish before pointing to a small blue blob north of the forest. "There is a lake not far from the tree line, and a lake means moisture, and moisture means mushrooms!" He closed his eyes and shivered with excitement, then hurried onward, Bauble lighting the path. "Delicious, delicious mushrooms!"

"Meat, you feathered fool! Meat! Haunch and marrow and grissstle and grease!" Snabla shrieked and slobbered, leaping to his feet and giving chase.

Hugo ignored him, barreling through the trees. Then he paused, just briefly, and glanced over his shoulder at Zelli, the glint in his eye and the tilt of his head a silent question. *Coming?* he seemed to ask.

Zelli told herself she could keep them safe. She told herself

there would be a time when she could slip away and find Allidora Steelstrike on her own. But until then, until her moment came, maybe it was not so bad to travel with company.

"Coming?" Hugo called back, in earnest this time.

"Coming," Zelli replied, joining kobold and owlbear and mimic in the humbling crush of dark, tall trees.

6

"**S**o that was the Endless Forest. Sort of thought it would be, I don't know, more . . . endless." Zelli pulled off her heavy pack to give her shoulders a rest, rubbing at them while she turned to survey the way they had come. A narrow path that had been visibly opened in the trees sealed itself even as she watched until at last the oaks formed a solid, impenetrable bulwark, the mountain of the academy just a vague smudge against the darkness.

"Actually, we can navigate it just fine," Bauble piped up, still masquerading as a lantern and now held high in the air by Hugo. "There is a fascinating history of the academy itself in the library, but I suppose none of you have read it. I practically have it memorized! The forest recognizes those who are welcome, and allows us passage,

but anyone else will wander and wander for days until, well . . ."

Snabla drew his claw across his throat and made a juicy croaking sound. "Mussst Snabla remind you of his unbearable hunger? Go, go, we hunt!"

The kobold trundled off toward the hint of reeds and water at the bottom of a gently sloped hill, his shield banging noisily on his back as he went. A slew of boulders dotted the way to the water, the long-abandoned remnants of a camp moldering to the left of the lake. From there, the ground rose again, a less dense, less intimidating line of trees cut to the east by a dirt path. Sprawling mountains pierced the sky still farther east, a thin halo of clouds ringing the topmost peaks.

"How did you know that?" Zelli asked the mimic as they set off after Snabla. "About the Endless Forest? I'd never heard that."

"I know everything about the academy!" Bauble chirped. "It's my favorite subject! Did you know that until two hundred years ago the mascot was the bulette?"

Zelli couldn't imagine why they would pick the bulette as a mascot. It was an ugly, burrowing creature, vicious and predatory, with razor-sharp teeth and a smooth, pointy head. Sure, it was

ferocious, but it was also *horrifying*.

"The academy council voted to change it after an *actual* bulette broke into the school and swallowed a third-grade kobold whole."

"That's grim," Zelli murmured.

"Flumphs are far more agreeable," Hugo agreed. "And flumphy."

They found Snabla at the water's edge, shield and bag discarded on the ground of the abandoned camp. The scene of a firepit was little more than a few stones and a charred smear, two leaning posts holding up a tattered rag of a tent.

"You and Bauble try to make a fire," Hugo directed, placing the "lantern" on the ground near Snabla. "Zelli and I will find what food we can at the forest's edge. This near to the lake, I'm sure we can find some edible tidbits."

"Fire! Yesss! Fire, of course!" Snabla perked up, rubbing his hands together feverishly. Then his eyeballs bulged, his gaze sliding back and forth between Hugo and Zelli. "Hmm, yes, how exactly to . . . When one tells Snabla to . . . After all, ssspent entire life in academy! Hmm, yes. Hmm . . ." The kobold leaned down and snatched up two twigs, then sawed them together, tongue poking out in concentration.

"Bauble?" Zelli gestured to the mimic.

"I'm not really fire," they said—a little haughtily, in Zelli's opinion. "You would know that if you paid attention in biology!"

"Here, then." She reached into her bag and tossed the flint she had packed to Snabla. "Strike it against a stone on top of some dry leaves."

Helpfully, Bauble immediately transformed into a handcart, the narrow brass edges of the lantern elongating and then curving, panes becoming the wooden sides and bottom of the cart.

"No problem," Bauble told them, wheels blinking.

"Shall we?" Hugo inclined his head slightly, then made for the scattered, barren trees beyond the lake. The water lapped quietly at the reeds and stones, a bright, fat moon hanging above the mountains to the east. Zelli looked over her shoulder, expecting to see Dungeon Academy there, a beacon, a talisman, but it could no longer be seen. A shiver ran through her.

"Oh, look!" Hugo's excited cry tore her out of her melancholy. He had a bouncy, boisterous run, his size making the ground shake beneath their feet as he ran to a glint of metal among the forest bushes.

"A hunter's trap, maybe," Zelli suggested, finding that a rudimentary mechanism had managed

to snare a hare. It looked as if it had been there for a while, but she doubted Snabla would mind or even notice. She heard Hugo make a soft gagging noise above her. "Go look for mushrooms; I'll handle this."

"Thank you, Zelli."

She made quick work of the twine and plate, freeing the hare and stuffing it in her bag. Hugo's tall, silvery silhouette was just about to vanish among the trees, but she caught up, eyes roaming the ground, sweeping back and forth. "What am I looking for?"

"Look at the base of the trees and on the stumps," Hugo instructed. "Do not pick anything with red on it, or white gills, or something that looks like a skirt around the stem." He trilled with delight and bent down, claws digging up a small cluster of frilly mushrooms, a light gold in color. "Beautiful! These will do nicely! Perhaps I can find a few wild ramps; then we shall truly have a stew going...."

"I should have brought lantern Bauble; I can't see a thing...."

"Leave it to me, friend. I can see quite well in the dark."

Zelli nodded, and made herself useful by holding the edible treasures Hugo discovered among

the dank, dirty base of the trees and in the dry brush. It was amazing to watch him at work, so much so that for a moment she forgot why they were camping and foraging at all.

He must have noticed her silence, for Hugo collected one last mushroom, handed it to her, and then nodded for them to go back the way they had come. "Are you not afraid? To be alone out here with a vicious monster?"

"No." Zelli huffed a laugh. "Aren't you afraid of me? We're meant to kill each other, you and I. We're not meant to be foraging buddies."

"I have little patience for *meant to be*," Hugo told her. "I am meant to gobble up every scrap of flesh and bone I can get my claws on, yet the thought disgusts me. Snabla is meant to terrorize and Bauble is meant to deceive and devour. Do any of us seem suited to our purpose?"

"I suppose you're right," Zelli admitted, arms and bag full with plants, fungi, the hare, and even a round, heavy gourd. "I . . . really don't know what my purpose is anymore. For so much of my life, I just wanted to keep my head down and be ignored. I knew I wasn't a minotaur, but I also didn't feel like a human, and I knew I didn't belong in a maze somewhere smashing up adventurers. So what do I do? Where do I belong?"

"Right now you belong with us, I think." Hugo smiled as well as he could with his beak, his eyes soft and bright in the gloom. "You belong on this journey to find your people, and maybe when you have your answers, your purpose will be clear."

Zelli nodded, her face suddenly red and hot. Nobody had ever said anything so kind to her before, and the warm feeling it gave her was almost uncomfortable. And weird. It made her want to go on talking and say more, probably too much, and so she went quiet for a while instead. But what Hugo had told her *was* kind, so she spoke

up one last time before they reached camp and the tentative fire burning there. "If I do find any of the Steelstrikes, it will be too dangerous for the rest of you. Even if they realize I'm a human, I can't promise they will understand . . . this."

"This," Hugo repeated with a sigh.

Friendship. Zelli shrugged. "Traveling with you all. I might have to leave. For good. You know that, don't you?"

"Who can say," he murmured, "until your purpose is clear? Ah, the fire is ready. Let us prepare our impromptu feast."

Snabla's eyes practically popped out of his skull when he caught sight of the hare. Despite his deft claws, Hugo, with his distaste for meat, could not prepare the hare, but that little mattered, as Snabla simply burned the fur off and had his meal. Mounding a few coals to the side of the fire, Hugo scooped out the gourd's innards and then used it like a bowl, nestling it among the glowing coals and adding the plants and mushrooms they had found, finally adding a dash of lake water before letting it all meld.

"What do mimics eat?" Zelli asked, settling down against her backpack while they waited for their meal to cook. "Adventurers? Boots and all?"

Bauble had transformed back into what appeared to be their most comfortable form, a hefty book. Now that Zelli looked more closely at the cover, it appeared to be covered in runes, as well as a translated title, marking it as a comprehensive history of the academy itself.

"We can absorb all kinds of things," the mimic replied; their eyes, though worked into the patterns on the book, seemed to her defiant. "Like adventurers, for example, yes. Did you pay attention *ever* in biology?"

"That was rude, I'm sorry," Zelli told them, biting the inside of her cheek.

"I would ask what minotaurs eat, but I already know," the mimic sniffed. "Because unlike some people, I do my homework."

"Mysssteries" was Snabla's guess. "Riddlesss."

They laughed, and then Snabla swung around in the dirt to pick up his rickety shield, thrusting it high above his crooked ears. "Riddles like the one emblazoned on this ssshield."

Zelli couldn't imagine anything being "embla-zoned" on such a piece of junk, but before she said a word, the kobold had passed the shield toward her. It felt flimsy in her grasp, held together with hopes and dreams and a few loose nails. But along the curved inside edge, she noticed that there was indeed an inscription. Unlike the shield itself, the inscription looked deliberate and well done, in fine, bold script, like a fancy placard under a king's statue.

"'Through blazing threats, flames reveal the true dragon scales,'" she read. "Maybe the shield is enchanted somehow."

"That's what I keep telling him," said Bauble. "He might sort it all out if he spent more time in the library and less time feeling sorry for him-self."

"Not sssorry for self," Snabla spat, taking the shield back from Zelli and holding it protectively

against his chest. "Jussst impatient. Mussst prove myself worthy, worthy in my father's eyes, then a real shield I will have! Sneef the Unending's shield!"

Through blazing threats, flames reveal the true dragon scales

Zelli watched the little kobold hug his shield tightly, and felt a pang of sympathy—what would it take to impress Sneef the Unending? It had to hurt Snabla that his own father didn't think him important enough to wield his ancestral shield.

It was then that Hugo pronounced the cookery finished, and so the mimic absorbed a bit of the stew, and Zelli discovered that the most unlikeliest of creatures, a hulking, clawed, feathered owlbear, proved rather an excellent cook. When they had eaten their fill and Snabla sat burping and picking at his teeth with a few small leg bones, Bauble roused themselves from staring into the fire to say, "In every tale and every legend, an adventuring party needs a name. What will we be called?"

"We are not filthy adventurers! We are dungeon dwellersss," Snabla corrected them. "We

do not obssserve filthy human-elfy-dwarven customs."

"That is so ignorant," Bauble sighed, rolling their eyes. "It has nothing to do with elves or humans or anything, just legends, those who bravely go and dare."

"Bauble, I quite concur," replied Hugo, tucking a curved claw under his chin thoughtfully. "Perhaps we could each put forward a suggestion, then vote."

Zelli paled. She wished Hugo hadn't agreed to Bauble's idea—this was a party destined to split. Once she found the Steelstrikes, their journey together would be at an end. She only hoped that end wouldn't include violence.

"Snabla abstainsss," the kobold grunted, flicking away his bone toothpick. As he did, just as the sliver of picked-clean white landed in the grass, an earsplitting *ca-CRACK* shook them all to their feet.

"Lightning?" Hugo wondered aloud, but it didn't take long for them to notice the bright purplish-blue cloud spreading across the dip in the mountains to the northeast. "That's ... The village is that direction. Horntree."

"Then our glory awaitsss!" Snabla shrieked, taking up his shield and hurling it onto his back.

Zelli had to admire his courage—the last thing she wanted was to go wherever that sound had come from, but the kobold was already charging off, small and spitting and woefully unprepared, lacking even a decent shield, and yet he was ready to fight for his classmates. She wondered what a Steelstrike might think of such a display.

"Come! I will prove myself worthy! Come!" Snabla hopped up and down, kicking up dirt as he urged them toward the forest path. Zelli took one last look at the ominous purple cloud hovering in the distance, drew in a deep breath, and picked up her pack.

"He's right," she said, forcing a wobbly smile. "Tales and legends; we'll never be in either if we stay here in camp."

The solemn, winding path led steadily upward, through a thickening of twisted, corpse-like trees, past piles of bones picked clean by the watchful ravens in the branches above. Moonlight speared through the canopy, though they walked mostly in darkness, Bauble back in Hugo's pack, all of them deciding against the lantern and the attention the light might bring.

The smell of burning reached them long before the path widened into a sparsely cobbled road, long before they traveled beneath a spindly arch with the HORNTREE VILLAGE sign swinging sadly at its center, damaged, the name hanging by a single hinge and dangling over their heads at a sharp angle.

"Do you see our classmates?" Bauble asked, somewhat inconveniently positioned behind

Hugo's great furry shoulder.

Zelli couldn't find her voice to speak. She had never seen such devastation. Her first memory of a village belonging to her kind, and it was in ruin—houses abandoned; animals wandering in a startled panic; windows shattered and thatched roofs blackened with char; billowing gray smoke that swirled into the seething purple cloud hovering over them all.

"I don't see anyone," Hugo told Bauble softly.

"Gone," Zelli murmured. She picked her way forward, across the road and beyond a toppled merchant's stall to the nearest home, where she peered into the open door and found it empty. When she closed her eyes and concentrated, it was almost as if she could hear the screams of the family as they ran. "They're all gone."

She wandered, aghast, toward the heart of the village, feet dragging, following a trail of left-behind belongings—baskets and blankets, weapons and apples and cloth dolls and shoes. If the villagers had been forced to flee, why not take their things? In the square, she felt the haunting cold of a place once lively and vivid now deprived of all expected life. She could imagine dances there, and festivals, harvest feasts and busy

market days. Now there was nothing.

No, she thought, noticing a silver glimmer in the muck. Not nothing . . .

Wedged between two cobbles and nearly lost to the mud sat a bent silver cloak badge. She wiped off the mud on her own tattered cloak and inspected the design. Her heart sank to her boots. Two crossed swords with a snarling bear in the middle. She had seen just such a design on Allidora Steel-strike's baldric. The others were approaching, and Zelli swiftly stood and tucked the badge into her belt, turning to face them with what she hoped was a guiltless expression.

Hugo's eyes lingered on her for a long, long time.

"Find anything?" he asked.

"No." She shook her head. "It's so strange. They left everything behind. . . ."

Hugo shrugged off his satchel, letting Bauble get a good look at their surroundings. They made a soft cry of fear and, in a fright, turned immediately into a pocket watch. Then a chair. Then finally a potted plant.

Two leaves on the fern blinked up beyond Zelli's head, fixed on the purple cloud. "This is fell magic. Evil, evil magic. Something like . . . like . . ."

Everyone waited, silent.

"Like necromancy," Bauble whispered.

Even Snabla hissed and hid behind his shield. Monsters might not like adventurers and heroes and the like, but everyone—everyone—feared and despised necromancy. Zelli had grown up with tales of necromancers hiding skeletons under her bed, undead spooks and ghouls haunting many a child's bad dreams. Tampering with death was unnatural, and while the school put up with the eccentric Professor Gast and his identity crisis, no other necromancy was tolerated or even considered. Life was life, death was death, to meddle in such things threatened the understood order of the universe. Zelli's hands felt suddenly cold. Such things seemed so distant from their lives at the school, could it really have come so near to them? Yet what else but something truly evil would explain not only the disappearance of all these villagers, but also their classmates? A little hamlet like this would be no match for sixth-grade oozes, kobolds, and kuo-toa.

Unless it wasn't a necromancer at all but your family that caused this disaster.

Zelli placed her hand defensively over the badge hidden beneath her belt.

"What is thisss contraption? A mossst diabolical weapon?" Snabla had leaned down and

scooped up something silver and muddy. He held it up for them to see, turning it this way and that.

"It's just a fork," Zelli told him, relieved he hadn't found anything truly dangerous.

But Bauble scoffed. "Nonsense. That's a Dwarven Nose-Picker."

Zelli shook her head. "It's definitely a fork."

"*You* are failing half your classes," Bauble reminded her. "*I* have perfect scores in Ghostly Groaning and Other Unsettling Noises, Taking Care of Your Hoard, and How to Befoul and Offend. I think *I* know a Dwarven Nose-Picker when I see one, thank you very much."

"Right," Zelli sighed. "Dwarven Nose-Picker, then. My mistake."

"Look! Something! Sssomething else!" Snabla hopped up and down suddenly, racing off. Footsteps. He had found a deep trail of footprints. They led through the mud and north out of the village. Where the cobbles ended, visible puddles of purple and blue goo gathered, bubbling with their own heat or intensity.

"Evil," Bauble whispered again, now safely inside Hugo's bag and back on his shoulder. Even with that ominous warning, Snabla raced over to study one of the puddles, and nearly swiped one clawed finger through the mystery muck. "Do not

touch it!" Bauble cried.

"Bauble is right. It is like foraging—never, ever touch or eat what you cannot identify," Hugo said sternly.

"I can't say what magic was used here. But I know it's not something we should play with." Bauble's ferny leaves shivered in the backpack.

"Then we follow," Snabla declared, leading the way out of the village and toward the densely packed footprints in the mud.

"Look at how many there are," Zelli breathed. "It's like the whole village just left altogether at once."

"And there," Hugo added, the four of them now returning to the familiar gloom of the woods. "Those are kobold tracks."

"Yesss, my kind! Our kin! We are on the right path!" Snabla ran alongside those tracks in particular, and in such a hurry that the others were forced to rush to keep up.

"Are you all right?" Hugo asked.

Zelli wondered if she looked as sick and afraid as she felt. "We just need to press on."

In truth, she didn't know how to answer. The

badge she had found could mean anything—that the Steelstrikes had left with the villagers, that one of them had come and already been slain, that they had passed through on some other adventure, or that they were in fact the evil force to blame for the purple cloud and the odd puddles. It occurred to her that even if they were her blood, she truly did not know anything about them. They could be far worse than anything learning to lurk or hoard or cackle at the academy.

It was foolish to leave the school. I hope we have enough training to survive this.

She tried to take heart, even if a more sensible corner of her heart said it would be wise to turn back. "If there are kobold tracks, then that means our classmates could be alive and well," she said. "We could still save them."

"Aye, we could," Hugo agreed, smiling and cheered by that. "Slow down, Snabla! That silly kobold is going to get into trouble if he goes off without us!"

"Snabla!" Zelli called. They had lost sight of him, the muddied tracks less certain now, covered and concealed here and there by the wild grass and brush of the forest. The moon rose higher, clearing the purple fog above the village, but its light brought small comfort as she, Hugo, and

Bauble crashed through the trees and into a clearing, where Snabla had gone very still, his shield raised in defense.

A single, high howl cut the silence. It was a lonely call until it wasn't, until a dozen other voices all joined it, a chorus of gathering wolves. Wild creatures in the woods and caverns and mountains of Faerûn were not like the monsters of the academy—they had no love for anyone trespassing on their turf, ogre, dwarf, kobold, or otherwise. They would fight and kill each other, and they would most certainly attack four wayward students.

The first yellow eyes appeared at the edge of the clearing, then one immense, furred paw, and the next, claws, and teeth and snouts coming next. Snabla retreated toward them, shivering, bumping into Hugo's knee and giving a sharp squeal of fright. Something small and soft tumbled into the clearing, but Zelli couldn't see quite what it was, because the wolves had come, in number and force, filling the space around them with gnashing fangs and tearing claws.

"Hugo!" Zelli cried, taking the wooden sword from her back and brandishing it at the nearest beast. "We need you! You're big enough to fight them!"

But when she glanced up at the owlbear, he had frozen, his beak parted slightly in terror, his eyes shut tightly against the danger. He trembled and raised his feathered, muscled arms, but only to cower, only to hide his face.

"I cannot," he stammered. "Forgive me, forgive me! I cannot draw blood!"

They were surrounded, and the first wolf leapt, swiping at Snabla and knocking his shield uselessly to the ground.

I brought them all here, Zelli thought, the sword heavier and heavier in her hands. *I brought them here, and for what? For the wolves. To perish.*

"Don't show the wolves your backs!" Bauble yelled from inside Hugo's bag. "To me!"

Zelli was already squashed up against Hugo's side, but she squashed herself harder, and so did Snabla, looking strange and forlorn without his signature shield. *What would Bauble transform into?* she wondered. *A bear? A trap? A tornado of terrible knives?*

Hugo's bag tipped over then, Bauble toppling to the ground, transforming before they landed into a small, round, ridiculous tambourine.

"Oh no." Zelli raised her sword. "We're doomed."

8

"**P**ick me up!" Bauble shrieked, rattling and jangling along the forest floor. "Pick. Me. Up! Please! Hurry!"

The wolves seemed to hesitate, and that was good enough for Snabla, who dove for the tambourine and took it up, raising Bauble above his head like a mighty magic orb and not a bit of hide, wood, and bangles.

"Shake me! Shake me at the wolves! The sound will frighten them, do it now, Snabla!"

"Thisss is humiliating," the kobold moaned, but did as he was told, banging his gnarled fist against the instrument, Bauble grunting in pain with each thump.

Shhh-ksh-OUCH!-shing-ch-shing-OOF!-clangity-HEY!

Zelli couldn't believe what she was seeing—the

banging and the noise actually worked. The wolves shied, showing their teeth, yellow eyes glowing with hungry intent, but gradually their shaggy gray heads bowed, and their tails lowered, and one by one they began, slinking back toward the edge of the forest, finally disappearing into the shrubs clustered at the edge of the clearing.

"Keep rattling me now and then," Bauble said, sounding winded. Two golden half-moons at the top of the instrument grew opaquer, the lower edge of the drum lifting to form lips. "The wolves will circle but the noise will frighten them away."

"Good thinking," Zelli told them, keeping her sword out and ready just in case. "And lucky that you pay attention in class the way you do. . . . You saved us, Bauble."

Hugo remembered how to move at last and crumpled to the ground. "Yes, you saved us, Bauble, and I failed you all. What good is a cowardly owlbear? What good is an owlbear who cannot thrash and bash, or tear with the sharpest of beaks and claws? Oh, I am sorry, my friends. I am sorry."

"Don't be so hard on yourself!" Bauble tried to say, but Snabla had already run off with the

mimic, toward the shaking bundle of fur rolled up and forgotten by the wolves, left there to shiver in the cold stillness of the clearing.

"Bauble is right," Zelli said, carefully placing a hand on the owlbear's shoulder. He hid his face and tried to shrug her off. "They are. You just panicked. This is our first time outside the school; none of us knew what to expect."

"I just . . . froze. Oh, do not hate me, Zelli. Please, do not hate me! I cannot change my nature, not all at once."

She grinned and then watched him climb slowly to his knees. "We survived. And even if we hadn't, I don't think my ghost would hate you. Much."

The owlbear chuckled softly and sniffled, and then they were both distracted by Bauble's sudden elated cry.

"By Bane's Black Hand, a blink dog! It's a blink dog!" Bauble exclaimed, rattling with percussive joy. "How exciting!"

"A blink dog, yesss, exciting and most deliciousss!" Snabla licked his chops, bending to scoop up the runty pup. It was yellow and orange, blending at times, with soft, tufted ears and a curiously long tail. Before Snabla could touch it, it disappeared, vanishing with a quiet pop.

It reemerged right
in front of Zelli and
Hugo, startling them
both. Before Hugo could
even gasp, it had licked
a slobbery stripe up the
owlbear's cheek.

"There, there now."
Zelli chuckled. "Cheer up,
Hugo. It likes you!"

"Because we saved it," Bauble said, now returning in the hands of Snabla, who rolled his beady
eyes and huffed.

"But he is not friend! He is food!"

"*She* is most certainly a friend," Bauble replied,
jingling all the while. "We can't hurt something so
sweet; she's all alone, and must have gotten separated from her parents! I think we should call her
Flash."

As if to agree, the pup vanished and then reappeared on top of Hugo's head, just as he began to
stand, then popped into the air near Snabla, banging her wiry tail against the flat of the
mimic's tambourine body, beating out
a merry little rhythm.

"Flash it is," Zelli said. She had
to admit, she *was* terribly cute.

"Though I'm not sure she's any safer with us. See? The footsteps lead that way."

They began their tracking again, though Snabla pouted, chin jutting out, his already cockeyed ears drooping as he stomped along at Zelli's side. He wasn't exactly being subtle about it, thumping Bauble every few steps to keep the wolves at bay, though the motion struck her as strictly perfunctory. She would have thought the mischievous creature would have taken great pleasure in any excuse to rattle and bop the mimic.

"Well, what is it?" Zelli asked, gazing down at the kobold. The blink dog, Flash, had settled onto Hugo's shoulders, hitching a ride, her tail curled around his wide neck.

"What will other koboldsss say when they learn that Snabla let feast become friend? Snabla will be dummy-dumdum to all kobold kind! Laughing sssock!"

"Stock," Bauble corrected him with obvious relish.

For that, Snabla gave them an extra-energetic bop.

"What does it matter what they think?" Hugo asked, peering across Zelli's shoulders and down at the kobold as they left the clearing behind, closely following the wending trail of footsteps

of varying sizes into the thick, close gloom of the forest. A smattering of yellow eyes regarded them, but the wolves kept their distance. "We know you, Snabla. And we know that you are not a dummy-dumdum. You did not hesitate at all when faced with the wolves, and you showed true bravery."

"Pah!" the kobold shrieked. "Kobold ssshould always be needling and poking, ssslicing and sticking! Never friendly! Never kind!"

Hugo frowned and opened his beak to continue, but Zelli shook her head surreptitiously at him. More gentle encouragement was not what the kobold needed. No, Snabla required his own unique manner of reassurance.

"Well," Zelli sighed. "I think you're perfectly wretched and terrifying, but what do I know?"

Snabla swung around to face them, and his eyes grew wide, glossy and tremulous with hope. "You . . . You do?" He curled one claw under his narrow, scaly chin. "Minotaur thinksss Snabla is wretched?"

"Um, oh yes. Absolutely dreadful," Hugo added with a single nod of his feathered head, catching on. "Horrid, harrowing, and hideous."

"The pokiest poker and sliciest slicer," Zelli continued, then leveled a sharp look at Bauble as

if to say, *Now you go. Come on.*

Bauble's lips would have been pursed if the mimic could show that expression as a tambourine, that much Zelli knew. At last, with Snabla still contemplating this sudden turn, the mimic muttered, "The unfriendliest fiend. The unkindest kind of kobold."

Thank you, Zelli mouthed behind Snabla's head.

Easing his pointy shoulders back, Snabla grinned and whacked the tambourine against his hip. "Party agrees: Snabla is ssstill horrible. Blink dog not-snack can ssstay."

At that, Flash let out a tiny, sleepy "Awoo!"

"Do you think she understands us?" Zelli asked, reaching up to move a branch out of the way as they forced their way deeper into the woods. She noticed a thin coil of smoke threading up from above the canopy, but when she gave it a second look, she noted that it was not pale gray but the unsettling warning hue of a bruise.

"No, obviously. Come on, Zelli, blink dogs only understand Sylvan," Bauble informed them. "I would ask what grade you all received in Common Creatures and Crawlers, but I'm afraid I already know the answer. . . ."

"There, the purple smoke. I see it again up

ahead." Zelli pointed, and they all slowed to a stop. She wasn't prepared to go charging headlong out of the forest; for the moment they had concealment, and that gave them the advantage.

Hugo excavated his map from his pack, brushing off a few errant herbs and mushrooms. Squinting at it in the shadowy dark of the woods, he let it snap back into a roll before returning it to his bag. "There's a ridge ahead, Bonebreak Gully, with a ravine just on the other side of the cave." He groaned. "Hence the name."

"We might be right out in the open." Moving carefully through the brush, Zelli leaned against a narrow, dead tree at the edge of the woods, before the ground plunged down into the gully, and then to the sheer drop of the ravine beyond. The tracks trickled toward lower ground, curving, leading toward the mouth of a tall, yawning cave. And walking into the cave, calmly, in a perfectly orderly fashion, went a stream of humans, dwarves, half-elves, and halflings, all manner of folk, old and young and oldish and youngish.

Snabla gave the tambourine one last bang before falling silent.

"That's Patty!" Bauble gasped, and without the benefit of hands, clarified, "The bugbear at the back! And see? There's Gutrash!"

"Your truuuuessst love," Snabla teased.

"Hush," Bauble muttered. "I had Bartering with him spring semester."

Just as Bauble had said, a strangely docile bugbear in spiked armor and furs brought up the rear of the line. Ahead of her, nearly swallowed by the mouth of the cave, was a similarly compliant goblin boy, his greenish ears sticking out of a domed helmet. Was a Steelstrike somewhere down there, hypnotized and quelled just like the others?

"They must be ensorcelled," Hugo whispered. "Enchanted somehow. Patty would never behave this way. Gutrash I really can't speak to, but given the name, I find it unlikely. . . ."

"Foul magicsss," Snabla hissed. "What do we do?"

For some reason, they all paused and looked to Zelli. She swallowed a squeak of fear and reached for her sword once more. She watched a dazzle of strange lights flash from the cave mouth, a spectacular display and dangerous promise of what they might face. Glancing at them each in turn, she felt, for just a moment, oddly at peace. They had come far together, survived hunger and wolves, and now their destination was clear.

"We need to get a closer look at that cave,"

she told them. "We need to put an end to whatever evil lies within."

9

S he had happy memories of the academy. Many, in fact. Zelli remembered being eight years old in the Lurkery, the practice forest on the academy grounds where students went to train their, well, *lurking*.

Usually the Lurkery was filled with young monsters playacting as adventurers so as to make the chase more realistic—slimes wearing mops for wigs and buckets for helmets, gnolls with long, bristling ferns draped over their muzzles to look like dwarves, and myconids with flimsy fake feet (or even upside-down hands) strapped to their mushroom stumps. But a long, humid summer descended, and all her fellow students had gone home to mother goblins and father flail snails, leaving only the children of professors and staff to run barbarously through the dungeon halls.

Zelli remembered squealing with laughter as her mother Kifin hunted her through the practice maze, the ground quaking with each inexorable step of the minotaur, Zelli shrieking at her to slow down and stop, that it wasn't fair. But Kifin laughed, too, and kept following her, chasing her with the inevitability only a minotaur could exude.

That was their whole thing. Inevitability.

Pigtails flying, Zelli finally rounded a hedge and almost slammed headlong into her mother, but the minotaur anticipated her, and caught her, and swung her up onto strong, familiar shoulders.

"My horn is crooked, Mama!" she remembered shrieking.

"Hush, let me see." Kifin had put her down and righted the horn, then poked her daughter gently on the nose. "You must be so careful, small one. You must never let anyone see you without your horns or your tail."

"Because I'm not like you," young Zelli had whispered, eyes wide with fear.

"No, you are like me, and like your mother

Iasme. You are already determined, and in time you will grow tall and strong, and you will fight with a minotaur's heart, and swing with a minotaur's fists. You are one of us, daughter, and you always will be."

"But—"

"Hush now." Kifin had taken Zelli's hand, cradling it carefully in her far, far larger palm. "Let us return to Iasme. Supper will be ready, and you know how cross she becomes if we return when it has gone cold."

I must really be in danger, Zelli thought now, inching closer to the mouth of the cave with Hugo, Snabla, Bauble, and Flash right on her heels. *Memories flashing in front of my eyes. . . .*

She remembered her first day of class. Everyone in her first period (Introduction to Hoarding) seemed to inhale as one as the professor announced a minotaur would be joining them. Minotaurs were rare, and there were no others currently enrolled at Dungeon Academy. Then everyone swung around to see her there, and once they saw how short, scrawny, and unimpressive Zelli looked, their interest immediately evaporated. She was the biggest disappointment of that semester.

At least I was the biggest something.

"Are you all right?"

Hugo's immense round eyes blinked down at her. Zelli snapped out of it, glancing up at the furry owlbear with a strained grimace. "Just . . . This is going to be really dangerous. Really, really dangerous. Are you afraid?"

"Yes," he said simply.

"Right." Zelli nodded. "Me too."

"We're nearly there."

And so they were. Snabla seemed the readiest of all, practically hopping out of his scaly skin with unsuppressed excitement, shield at the ready, one tiny fist raised, balled, and poised to strike. At the mention of their journey drawing to a close, Bauble made a choked squeaking sound, then transformed into a blanket. They couldn't hold that shape, shivering and jangling, a tambourine once more. The cave loomed, a cascade of disorienting pale purple lights flickering from inside, so far within the system that only the dullest roar of spells and voices reached them. A foul, wet worm smell leaked from the cave mouth, but the villagers and monsters who were magicked into walking calmly together didn't seem to notice.

"It's like they're sleepwalking," Zelli said, leaning over to wave her hand in front of a seemingly contented dwarf, who had left the house in his nightclothes, one slipper missing on his hairy, lumpy foot.

"Whoever did this must be very powerful," commented Bauble. They reverted to their bookish form, the wolves now a distant and forgotten

danger when faced with the unknowable terror waiting somewhere inside the cave system.

They all paused a moment to observe the line of villagers and monsters, and Zelli could only guess what the others were thinking, but she had an inkling that they shared her fear. She could see Snabla's little shoulders shaking as he held his rickety shield up in front of him, just in case. There was a quiet rattling behind them, and for an instant Zelli was convinced Bauble had changed into another form, swinging around to find a very convincing skeleton standing there behind her. Even as she watched, the skeleton became steadier, then leered at them, jaw askew, its skull and femur and finger bones dripping with the odd purple ooze.

"Bauble!" Zelli grinned, amazed that the mimic could do such a thing. "That's terrifying. I'm impressed, I had no idea mimics could—"

"Zelli? Z-Zelli?" Bauble's voice came not from the skeleton rattling toward her, but from Hugo's head. Her heart falling and her pulse rising, Zelli leapt back and spun around again, this time finding Bauble, now an immense floppy hat, covering the owlbear's entire head.

"That's not me!" Bauble squeaked through a fold in the hat. "I'm right here! Cowering in fear!"

"Look out!" Zelli shrieked, swinging her sword

at what was certainly *not* Bauble.

The skeleton veered out of the way of her jab on unsteady, spindly legs, then leapt toward Hugo with its fingers curved like claws.

"What is going on? Someone tell me!" Hugo cried, trying to pull Bauble off his head.

"A skeleton is coming right at us!"

After his moment of hesitation in the woods, Zelli expected him to flounder, but this time Hugo puffed out his chest and stood his ground, snatching the hat off his head, and as the skeleton threw itself toward him, the owlbear swatted him down, the necromanced foe shattering to pieces.

"Necromancy," Bauble whispered, melding back into the shape of a book. "That's not good."

"What isss on feathers?" Snabla asked him, pointing at a smudge of purple near Hugo's right elbow, right where he had slammed into the skeleton. He frowned and picked at it, tearing out the feathers there.

"I do not know," Hugo stammered. "But I shan't let it linger there."

"Does it hurt?" Zelli watched as his silvery-white feathers fluttered to the ground, landing on the broken remains of the skeleton.

"No," the owlbear sighed, and wiped his palm and claws on a fern at the base of the cave. "It feels

like nothing at all."

"We should hurry," Bauble pointed out. "Almost everyone is inside the cave, and we need to find out what's controlling them!"

Snabla began to march right in next to the line, but Hugo grabbed him by his tunic and yanked him back. "We should exercise caution. There

could be hundreds of skeletons like that one!"

"We can't just stand out here doing nothing," Bauble replied crossly. "Those students are in danger!"

"What if we pretend?" Zelli had been doing that all her life and had become somewhat proficient at it. She thought again of being chased by her mother through the Lurkery; somehow that hadn't felt like pretending. That had felt like she really was a minotaur, really part of something. A family. "We could just join the line, pretend like we're zonked out and magicked like the others."

They all turned to consult Bauble, who had quietly become the resident expert on such things.

"It's the best plan we have," the mimic admitted with a shrug. "Here, Hugo, pick me up. You all do what the villagers are doing, and I'll keep watch from your bag."

"Snabla say we charge! Snabla fight ten thousand ssskeletons!"

"Forget the skeletons," Zelli told him, joining the line and fixing a dull-eyed, dreamy expression on her face. Hugo did the same, and in they went. On the outside she might have appeared calm, but inside, her thoughts were a messy tangle, as twisted and

knotted as her stomach. She was about to risk her life, and the lives of others, just for the chance to see and know her real mother. Would it really be be worth it?

What if Steelstrike had already moved on? Worse still, what if she had been magicked, too, and they would have to save her? How would she explain to her friends that they needed to help a disgusting *human*?

She tried not to let the terror show on her face. "It will take all of our bravery to fight a necromancer. You'll get your chance, Snabla. We'll all get our chance."

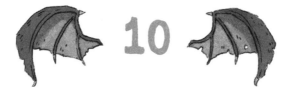

10

The plan worked, and Zelli silently congratulated herself on at least getting them safely inside the cave, no small feat when risen skeletal sentinels stood vigilantly watching. Though she kept her eyes forward, she glimpsed that some were obviously adventurers who had met their misfortune in the cave—wearing loose travelers' garments and satchels with ropes, skulls cracked from an unlucky fall. And she could see why—the cave itself reminded her of a honeycomb: a web of thin, interconnected bridges, a perilous, precarious terrain to navigate even for the most careful adventurer.

Hugo, with his huge and somewhat clumsy feet, nearly slipped as they crossed the

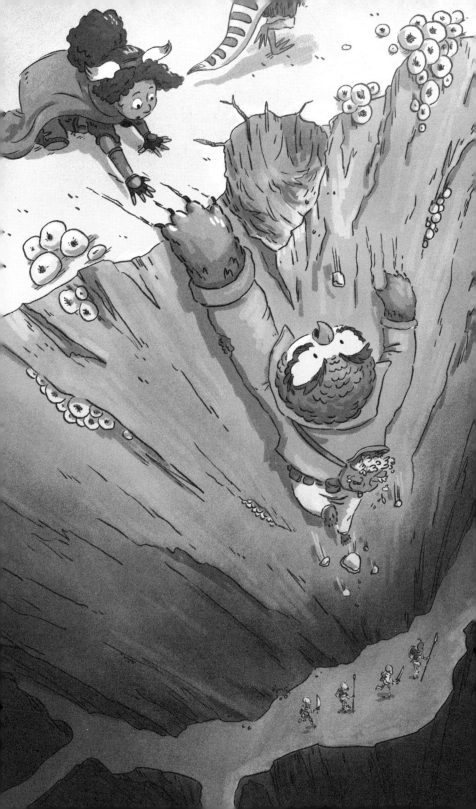

very first bridge, a cascade of pebbles shimmering down into the unseen depths.

"It's just like the path down to the dungeon classrooms," she murmured out of the corner of her lips. "Keep steady and don't look down."

But Zelli didn't quite keep her own advice, glancing at the stomach-churning drop just inches to her right and left. Torches blazed along their trail, some held by the skeletons, others sticking out of ancient, rusting sconces. The wet smell was chased away by the stench of whatever noxious fuel burned in the torches, while occasional bursts of violet light surged up from well below their feet. A filmy, glistening pattern clung to the ceiling, the high corners of the cave packed with what looked like pitted, bulging spider eggs.

The skittering, chittering chatter coming softly from everywhere and nowhere told her there were more than just skeletons and necromancers present, and she wondered how many of those dead adventurers had met a sticky, cocooned end.

The cave's bridges disappeared into shadowy corridors, while their path led ever downward, the temperature dropping precipitously as they wound their way deeper inside. After a while, Zelli began to notice that the skeletal sentinels were no longer present, concentrated at the cave mouth, no doubt there to guard against folk like them coming to rescue the villagers and monsters.

She hazarded a quick glance in every direction, finding they were no longer being watched. Well, not by any magicked skeletons, at least.

"Hey," she whispered. "Hey!"

Hugo slowed down, then took Snabla by the shoulder. Flash and Bauble peered out from the satchel on Hugo's back, the little hound's tongue and tail wagging with anarchic glee.

"Look," she whispered, pointing to a fork in the stone bridges up ahead. "The skeletons are all behind us, and I think we can find a faster way down."

The villagers and monsters were walking at a plodding speed, but if she and her friends arrived last, then it might be too late to stop whatever mischief was going on below. Zelli carefully inched her way around Hugo and Snabla, choosing wisely not to look down, then dashed to the left, taking a short jump onto a separate, narrow stone outcropping that then dipped down, running parallel to and then scooping under the bridge holding the villagers.

"Careful, Hugo," she called.

"I don't know how strong these stones are."

Snabla tossed himself across the divide recklessly, landing in a scaly heap beside her. The blink dog teleported across the gap, settling on the other side on Zelli's back. They all watched as Hugo swung his arms back and forth a dozen times, working up the courage and momentum to take the jump. Backing up, Zelli and Snabla watched as he grunted and leapt, a brief victory expression wiped clean by the unmistakable sound of stone splintering beneath their weight.

"Hurry! Slide down!" Zelli grabbed Flash and clutched the fuzzy thing to her chest, blindly throwing herself down the steep, smooth stone, which carried her in a curved path to the right, through a thin, disgusting gauze of spiderwebs to a wider, safer landing cluttered with seething eggs.

Zelli stood up just in time to feel Snabla, Hugo, and Bauble in Hugo's bag slam into her legs from behind. They toppled to a stop in a heap, Flash helpfully blinking out of existence before popping herself onto Hugo's head, the wiggly cherry on top of a slimy sundae.

Yanking herself free of the others, Zelli climbed to her feet and wiped at the spider silk and cave muck covering her mail and jerkin.

"Don't disturb the eggs," came Bauble's choked, frightened voice from inside Hugo's pack. "If I'm right, those are sword spider clutches. We don't want to tangle with those. I mean, it's right there in the name—they might be furry and striped, but those sharp ridges on their legs are deadly, and their bite is venomous, too! Just one drop of that venom would be enough to kill any of us."

"Nasssty." Snabla stuck out his tongue and backed away quickly from the nearest cluster of gooey, pulsing egg sacs. A shiver scraped down Zelli's spine, and she hurried to the edge of the platform, desperate for a way to move on.

"It looks like someone cobbled together a rope crossing," she said, squinting into the gloom now that they were away from the skeletons and torches. "There. I see a rope on the other side, but it's much too far to reach."

"Might you turn yourself into a bridge?" Hugo asked Bauble.

The book in his pack sighed. "Not one that big! I'm only twelve!"

Before they could hurl more suggestions at

Bauble, Flash stirred on Hugo's head, giving a small, curious yip before vanishing. She appeared on the other side of the gap, wagging her tail and staring at them, head cocked to the side curiously.

"Yes!" Zelli shout-whispered. "Good girl! Get the rope! Free the rope for us!"

She mimed clutching the rope with both hands, then swinging, then doing the same with her leg

Swoooshhhhh

hooked around the rope, too.

Hugo and Snabla did the same, pointing and gesturing and whispering feverishly while the dog simply wagged her tail faster and faster.

"She thinks this is hilarious," Hugo sighed.

"She's not wrong," Zelli replied.

The dog finally seemed to notice the tattered end of the rope dangling not half a foot from her snout. Delightedly, she lunged for the end of it, then began tugging at it and growling, playing her own kind of game with it.

"Brilliant," Hugo muttered. "Now what?"

"Give her a moment," said Bauble, pulling themselves further outside Hugo's bag.

"We do not have a moment," he reminded them. "The fate of our classmates is at stake; who knows what these necromancers intend to do!"

At last, Flash let go of the rope, and it swung out across the gap, not with any great speed, but enough for Zelli to scramble to the edge and catch it, nearly plummeting into the pit. Hugo and Snabla each grabbed an ankle, hoisting her away from certain doom.

"Thanks," she said, exhaling on a yelp. Then she pulled herself up on the rope and prepared to swing. "What matters is we got there eventually."

One by one, or two by one, in Hugo and Bauble's case, they swung across the divide, regrouping on the other side. The ledge elongated into another narrow bridge, carrying them steeply downward again, the walls and ground slick with moisture, the presence of spiderwebs and eggs lessening as it became colder and evidence of adventurers past became more prevalent. Snabla rushed forward to trip and disarm what appeared to be a rudimentary trap, probably left to protect against the spiders.

"Ha!" Bauble laughed as the kobold fussed with the old spike trap. "That looks just like my retainer."

"Grossss," sniffed the kobold, poking out his tongue.

They found evidence of an old campfire, too, and a mostly disintegrated bedroll. A few coins, bloodied, were scattered near the camp.

It didn't hold their attention for long; they had traveled deep enough into the cave to discover where that long, long line of adventurers and monsters was going. A bright, persistent purple light shone from the precipice up ahead. They huddled at its edge, Flash now safely back in Hugo's bag with Bauble, sneaking in a happy puppy lick here or there, much to Bauble's chagrin.

"Stop!" Bauble would grouse. "You'll make my pages curl!"

The bridge holding the villagers wound in a lazy spiral until at last it ended at the very bottom of the cave. There, the darkness and gloom was banished by the glow of a towering portal, its oval surface like the perfect, unrippled glass of a mirror, though the color of wolfsbane. A dozen or so skeletons stood guarding the contraption, their skulls as blank as the faces of those forced into entering the portal.

Through this magical gateway, the villagers disappeared one by one, stepping into the unknown, each teleported body making a hushed, warped sound, like the zip of a bee careening past one's ear.

"Where are they going?" Hugo gasped, covering his beak with both hands.

"Do you hear that?" Zelli asked, ignoring him, for she did not have the answer, nor was she keen to speculate. "It sounds like . . . like . . ."

"A battle! It could be our classmatesss! At lassst!" Snabla scrambled away, along the edge closest to the portal on the flat floor of the cave below. The others hurried after him, passing under the narrow bridge where the villagers and monsters shuffled along. As they reached the outcropping and the remains of another camp, the commotion became clearer—two raised voices. Two contenders locked in battle.

"They are not our peers; that is a human!" Hugo whispered excitedly.

"And a necromancer," Bauble added, with decidedly less enthusiasm.

They were both correct—below, a stone's throw

from where the portal glistened and buzzed, a tall, gaunt figure in rune-embroidered black robes lifted a staff high, a shock of pale green light bursting forth from it. The human he fought dodged out of the way, low to the ground, a hefty double-handed sword at the ready, her cloak flashing around her as one of the necromancer's skeletons lurched toward her, scattered to dust by the force of her sword.

"It's not just a human," Zelli whispered, looking at the illustration from her textbook come to life. "It's a Steelstrike."

11

At once, she felt the pressure of Hugo's eyes on her. Zelli closed hers, turning away from her friends and from the battle raging below. She had seen the number of skeletons being risen and flung, risen and flung at Allidora Steelstrike, and she knew it was just a matter of time before the woman—the human, *her flesh and blood*—was overcome. Every clang of sword against bone made her startle, as if she herself had become brittle and then tender to the touch.

This was what she had come for, why she had fled the academy and her mothers in the first place, but at the moment of revelation, she felt only terror.

Her feet felt rooted to the stone, and then she sensed Hugo's big, warm presence at her side. He had left behind Flash and Bauble in his bag with

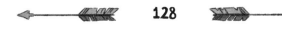

Snabla, and they all watched, gripped by the scene unfolding below.

"This is real now," Zelli murmured, hoarse. "That is an adventurer, someone we've been trained all our lives to hate and fight. I can't let you go down there. She might spare me and I can help her, but if she sees the rest of you . . ."

"You know we cannot let you do this alone," Hugo replied, his gentle voice a strange counterpoint to the violence screaming up at them from below.

"And yet you must." Zelli turned to face him, placing her hand on his shoulder and half smiling up at him. "Protect the others. I'm going to go help her."

"Zelli—"

But she had already returned to the ledge and drawn in the breath that would steady her for the words to come. "Snabla? Bauble? Flash?"

At first they didn't hear her, so she said their names louder. Snabla was the first to turn, and sneered at her.

"What is face? Looks like you sssaw a ghost."

"What is it, Zelli?" Bauble asked.

"I have to go down there," Zelli said, and put up her hand, hurrying before anyone could interrupt her, including Hugo, who waited at her back.

Still, Snabla and Bauble ignored her, making their opinions forcefully known.

"That is madnesss," blurted Snabla.

"The Dungeon Academy student handbook *clearly* states that interfering with any adventurers in the open is strictly forbidden unless first instructed to do so by a faculty or staff member. Section five, paragraph six, subparagraph b.

"You could get suspended! For, like, ever!" Bauble added, eyes wide with an overachiever's academic terror.

The kobold nodded along to each word. "What the mimic sssaid!"

"It doesn't matter. I'm going to help that human. Yes, even though she's an adventurer, no matter what the student handbook says. There's something you all need to know. . . ." She didn't expect it to hurt so much. It was one thing to leave them behind; it was another to betray their trust all along, and use that betrayal to chase them away. Trembling, Zelli reached up and pulled off her horns, tossing them to the floor between them.

She didn't look at their faces quite yet, afraid of what she might see there.

"I'm not a minotaur; I never was. My mother found me in a basket and raised me as a dungeon dweller. That human down there . . . she's my real mother, Allidora Steelstrike. I came here to find answers, to find her, and now I'm going to help her defeat that necromancer." Zelli sucked down another nervous breath and stumbled on, her hands in tight fists at her sides. "You can't trust me; you can't trust any adventurers or humans. We're your sworn enemies. Go back. Go back to the academy and don't get tangled up in this. Please. It's all right if you hate me, just go back. This is something I have to do on my own, as a human."

Snabla's underbite shook. "But we come so far—"

"Go back!" Zelli shouted. "I'm a human. You hate me! I'm everything you've been taught to fight and terrorize and kill. Get out of here!" Then

she reared back and roared at them, the most ferocious, guttural sound she could manage, pulling it from deep within her belly, knowing that if she didn't frighten them away, it could mean their lives.

They jumped back, startled, but nobody moved or retreated.

"Zelli," Bauble said softly. "We know. We've known for a while."

"Sssnabla is small but not stupid," the kobold added. He gave a snorting laugh and then waved Zelli off. "We know you are ssstinky human, but you could be stinkier. Snabla will fight with you; we will all fight with you. You brought us thisss far, no turning back now."

Zelli frowned, turning to each of them. "You really don't care?"

"You go help that adventurer, just as long as

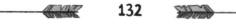

you help our classmates, too," Bauble replied while Hugo returned and hoisted them and Flash onto his back. Zelli didn't know a book could look determined, but in that moment, Bauble absolutely did. "We have your back, Zelli." As if to illustrate, Bauble's book grew a flapping cape. "Just, you know, tell her not to kill us?"

"Behold! Usss! Saving an adventurer and the mossst popular students at ssschool!"

"We better hurry," Hugo pointed out, gesturing to the mayhem of the battle, "or there won't be much of her to talk to."

The owlbear was right—the necromancer and his puppets had her cornered. As they watched, five skeletal warriors dove at Allidora Steelstrike, overwhelming her, slamming her to the ground while the robed necromancer drifted above her, the fluid hem of his robes floating just above the ground, a ghastly, icy mist gathering below him as he raised his staff high again, an ominous blaze of green light gathering at its tip. Steelstrike's sword tumbled out of her grip, spinning away uselessly, lost under a tide of skeletal feet.

"Release them, fiend!" the human cried, even while the skeletons piled on top of her. "I will not be the last to come! More will gather, more will fight you; such evil will never be allowed in this land!"

"Be silent. These servants are mine now, you witless worm. Soon every village and town from here to the Shining Sea will be overrun," he bellowed. "I command armies; my master commands legions! There are none here with the power to stop him. Every soul we capture is another for his army, and when we return in force, you shall be powerless against our vast legions. You will fall to your own allies, your own kin, all of them commanded by my lord."

"If that's true, we need to close that portal as quickly as we can," Bauble gasped. "We can't let Patty and Gutrash stay under the control of a necromancer!"

"It is t-too awful to contemplate," Hugo agreed.

"Then now!" Zelli thundered. "With me!"

Hugo squared his shoulders, even if his feathers remained ruffled with fear. The kobold no higher than the owlbear's knee raised his shield, ready to charge; Flash gave a low howl from Hugo's pack; and even Bauble managed a brave, war-worthy cry.

Zelli didn't know what to feel in that moment, charging into battle with her friends—her dungeon-monster-creature friends—rushing in to help her human adventurer mother. None of it made sense, but then, she thought, not much of

her life ever had. It was all mixed up, her heart, her past, her future, but she did know for certain that they had to stop the necromancer, that neither monster nor adventurer wanted anything to do with that kind of evil. Maybe it would only be a temporary alliance with the Steelstrikes or with her monster friends, but in that moment, she had allies, and she wasn't going to fight alone. All her life, her mothers had been preparing her for this moment—to stand tall and face down whatever adversity came to her. She tried to embody them, tried to feel nine feet tall and made of iron, with horns that could gore and hooves that could stampede. What she actually looked like, she didn't know, but she felt in her heart like her adopted mothers' daughter, a mighty minotaur.

She rushed down the steep, slippery slope toward the bottom of the cave, nearly losing her feet but letting the momentum carry her, training sword hefted over her head, her face twisted into a snarl as she hurtled toward her first real battle.

Her sword collided with the nearest skeleton, and the impact hit her not as a human, but as a minotaur. Swinging her weapon, throwing her weight around, she felt strong and sturdy and inevitable, just like her mothers had taught her to be. Surprise was on their side when it came to the risen warriors, and she bowled them over easily while Snabla lashed out with his shield at any that managed to get by her.

"My ssshield is impalatable!" Snabla cried, smacking into a skeleton's leg.

"Impenetrable, silly!" Bauble couldn't help but correct him, even in the heat of battle.

Zelli glimpsed the necromancer ahead, eyes locking with his, a cold whisper of death slicing through her as she beheld him—the dark hollowness to his sickly face, the pointed chin, and the strange marks carved into the flesh of his forehead ...

Behind them, the ground rumbled and rattled, and all the skeleton foes they had defeated rose again, commanded with a single nod by the necromancer. They were surrounded, Hugo and Snabla pressed into her sides, the sack on the owlbear's back trembling visibly.

"Oh, you very small fools," the necromancer chuckled. "I heard you coming with your tambourine song, with your clumsy steps and clumsier ideals. You are far too late to be of use, if you ever might have been at all. We will empty out the unsuspecting villages, sleepy and undefended, and then we will come for your academies and make soldiers of all you creatures—every last slime, dragon, and gnoll will serve!"

"Leave them be, Lord Carrion!" The woman to their left gathered her strength and rose to her knees. Zelli stared at her, in awe, in fear, watching a face just like her own seize with pain and then fight through it and continue. Allidora Steelstrike was a tall, imposing figure, even in defeat, even without her sword. Reaching into her belt, Zelli wrapped her hand around the Steelstrike emblem and told herself she wouldn't be afraid. "Fight me; I am your equal."

"No," Zelli called back, wiping sweat from her brow and jabbing her sword in Lord Carrion's direction.

"We fight together. Let our classmates go! Let them ALL go! We won't let you take them!"

The other human, Allidora, seemed distracted by Zelli as she looked at her. Perhaps it was a flicker of recognition in her eyes, or panic. Maybe the older human realized she was looking at almost a near copy of herself. There was no time for Zelli to consider it more, for Bauble suddenly spoke up.

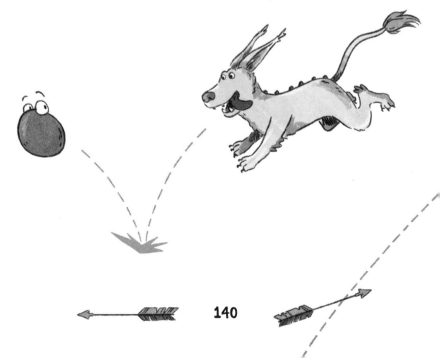

"I have an idea!" they yelled, then shrank down into a small red ball. "Toss me!"

Hugo frowned. "But—"

"Don't argue. Just toss me at a skeleton, Hugo!"

The owlbear did as he was told, and the genius behind Bauble's plan quickly became clear. As soon as the red ball was hurled at the nearest skeleton, Flash took notice and yipped with joy.

Flash popped out of Hugo's bag, appearing the next instant inside the rib cage of the skeleton closest to Allidora Steelstrike, trying to catch Bauble-the-ball but instead making the skeletal minion explode in a shower of bone fragments. Bauble bounced away before the pup could catch them, landing on top of another enemy. *Pop-pop-pop!* The blink dog vanished and leapt to the next skeleton and the next, chasing the Bauble ball, jumping from foe to foe until a path around Steelstrike had been cleared.

Pop

Pop

Pop!

Lord Carrion bared his teeth and flourished his staff, a blast of heat smacking them all in the face as a wall of towering flames surged up from the ground, protecting him from their blows. Bauble dodged back across the wall of fire, slightly singed, with Flash not far behind. They were soon back in Hugo's bag, Bauble, still smoking, returning to their book form. Many of the skeletons had been vanquished, but now they had an inferno to deal with.

"Bauble!" Hugo cried. "That was amazing!"

"I know. Look, we broke his concentration! He can't channel the portal while he creates that fire," Bauble squeaked from inside the sack. "It's Magic 101. From what I've read about necromancers, they are much weaker when their concentration is broken, losing their ability to control their minions or sustain difficult spells, which means—"

"We strike now!" Zelli agreed, racing forward. This was their best chance, even if it meant dealing with the heat from the fire.

And Bauble was proved right—the portal across the way, on the other side of the stone bridge, flickered, flashing unevenly before sputtering out entirely. A halfling girl clutching her dolly came to a confused stop just in front of it, then waited, still ensorcelled but safe for the moment.

Zelli slashed her way to the human, who gained her feet and sword, gathering her breath for a moment while more skeletons rushed from where the portal had been. As soon as Zelli came near, she saw the recognition in the woman's eyes. Up close, their resemblance was so obvious, so clear, that Zelli almost hiccuped in shock.

The other human noticed, too. Allidora Steelstrike stared at her, blood trickling from a cut on her forehead. "But—but you look like—"

"There's no time for that," Zelli told her, turning away, cheeks blazing. "We have to get through the fire somehow!"

Snabla, Hugo, and Bauble joined them amid the scattered bones, while Flash went on flashing, apparently enjoying herself too much to stop. The dog, however, could do nothing about the blazing fire separating them from the necromancer. Even if she got on the other side, Zelli thought, a pup was no match for a sorcerer of that power. Lord Carrion mumbled something softly to himself, the portal beginning to appear again, flickering back into existence. They were out of time to debate or hesitate.

"A kobold of worth knowsss when his time has come," Snabla suddenly said, snatching up his ramshackle shield and thrusting it out from his chest. It was as if to Snabla, he held a radiant golden shield, an emblazoned heirloom, priceless and ageless, the weapon of numerous heroes come and gone. It might have been made of precious metals and covered in jewels, it might have seen a thousand battles, it might have been the stuff of dreams. It was none of those things, but Snabla didn't seem to know or care; there was only the gleam of tales and glory in his eye.

"Behind me," cried the kobold, already sprinting on tiny intrepid feet toward the flames. "Into the fire we go!"

"**S**nabla! Snabla!" Zelli, Hugo, and Bauble shouted after him in unison. Flash disappeared, popping into the air and then across the flames, exploding another skeleton as she landed.

"Your shield won't hold!" Zelli cried, trying to reach the kobold before he sacrificed himself to the fire.

Hugo ran as fast as he could, each heavy step shaking the cave floor. "It is too flimsy, Snabla, wait! The wood will be consumed by the flames!"

Bauble tried to shout something, too, but Zelli couldn't hear it over her own frantic shrieking and breathing. Behind her, Allidora Steelstrike guarded their flank, sword slicing horizontally through two skeletons at a time as she slashed and slashed, seemingly with endless reserves of stamina. It was hard for Zelli to believe that she

was really fighting back-to-back with a legendary human adventurer, and her family, at that. They seemed to swing with identical technique, and shout with the same ferocious thunder.

"What is that little creature doing?" Allidora yelled to Zelli. "He's going to get himself killed!"

Zelli could hardly believe that a human was

expressing concern for a kobold, but maybe unexpected sympathies ran in the family. Or maybe Allidora realized these reckless children charging into the fray were her only chance to defeat the

necromancer, whatever the reason, so she was with them, at least for the moment. They both spun to follow in Snabla's wake, hurrying to catch up to him.

The flames banished the chill of the cave, and Zelli felt her cheeks grow hot, perspiration dotting her forehead as she tried to reach Snabla before it was too late. The kobold couldn't be stopped, and marched toward the fire without hesitation. "Wait! Snabla, wait!" Bauble's voice finally broke through the din just as they reached the wall of fire. The mimic transformed into a candle snuffer, a tiny vial of water, and then, with a quavering sigh, a book on forest fires. None of it, of course, was enough to help with the inferno. Behind the surging flames, the necromancer's power gathered, the portal nearly completely restored.

"Yes!" Lord Carrion shrieked, his voice like a blade rasping across ice. "Yes! Throw yourselves at the fire! Cinders! Ash! You will burn! Little fools. I will not be defeated by mere children! Not I, who has portaled across the Nether, not I, master of deep, dark places, lord over the undead, summoner unmatched!"

"The portal!" Allidora shouted when the necromancer had finally finished. "We cannot allow him to summon the portal!"

"We know!" Zelli, Hugo, and Bauble replied in harried unison.

"Snabla!" Hugo's voice rose above it all then as the kobold's shield felt the first searing kiss of flame, the flimsy, splintering wood immediately scorched, smoke filling the air around them. But it was too late. There came a dreadful silence, a gasp before the horrible fate revealed, but in that stillness Zelli finally heard Bauble whisper what they had been trying to say all along, only this time they said it in dazed wonder.

"The shield!" they shouted as Snabla miraculously stepped unharmed through the wall of flame, cutting a path for them and leaving the way open for his friends to follow. Before their eyes, the shield glittered and grew, wood becoming steel, steel becoming gilt, a hundred filigree dragon scales forming like icicles on a frozen eve. "Through Blazing Threats, Flames Reveal the True Dragon Scales!"

"Worthy!" Snabla raised the enchanted shield high above his head, the flames reflecting off its gold edges in blinding flashes. "I am worthy! Father knew! Father knew I would be worthy! Worthy of the great Sssneef!"

"Be silent!" Lord Carrion turned on the kobold, striking with the end of his staff. His spell disrupted, the portal fizzled out again, but the heavy wooden weapon connected hard with Snabla's shield, sending him flying and crashing to the floor. Dazed, Snabla tried to rise up again, but Lord Carrion's skeletons descended. Zelli, Hugo, and Bauble raced to defend him, forming a bulwark between him and the undead minions coming for their friend.

"We're coming, Snabla!" Bauble cried. "I'll turn into . . . into . . ."

The mimic made a strangled sound of frustration, able to manifest into no more than a bit of tattered bandage.

"It doesn't matter what you are," Hugo reminded Bauble as they ran. "He just needs us."

Allidora Steelstrike took her chance, eyeing the necromancer and preparing to strike, hoisting

her heavy blade to her shoulder before swinging with a hoarse scream, the last of her stamina bursting forth with terrible speed and force.

But Lord Carrion anticipated her, pulling a small black vial from his robes and drinking it in one gulp before tossing the thing away to shatter among shuffling skeletal feet. He raised his staff again, his strength only surging while Steelstrike's waned. With a quick twist of his fingers, the warrior froze, caught with her sword midair, a pale green haze encasing her entirely. After, the necromancer sagged, weakened, heaving for air. Zelli ran to the woman. Had the spell killed her? Or just stopped her in her tracks? Zelli looked for some sign of life but found none. The warrior wouldn't be helping them like that. She tried to imagine what Allidora Steelstrike would want her to do. It was right there in the name, wasn't it? Zelli rolled her shoulders back and tried not to think about losing Allidora just yet; instead, she reached for the woman's sword and tried to pull it free. She yanked and yanked, but the spell was too strong.

Maybe I wasn't meant to wield her sword.

Even without the sword, they couldn't give up.

"Now is our chance," Zelli said, turning away from Allidora with a hitch in her throat and helping

Snabla to his feet with a squeeze of his shoulder. "He should be too exhausted to cast more spells! Remember what Bauble told us? Break his concentration, stop him from casting spells."

"On the contrary," the necromancer panted, leaning heavily on his staff as Hugo led the charge. "I have one card yet to play."

Zelli watched in horror as Lord Carrion pointed his staff toward the owlbear, who stopped at once, as frozen as Allidora. He did not, however, remain still, the tiny, almost imperceptible spot of purple ooze near his elbow glowing like a brand before his kind eyes narrowed, suddenly filled with hatred.

ZNZNZ

Zelli had forgotten all about the blow Hugo had struck against the skeleton outside the cave, and that he had tried but failed to remove every trace of the blackish goo from his arm. She couldn't have guessed that even that infinitesimal amount was enough to give the necromancer power over her friend.

Hugo gnashed his beak and lashed out at them with lethal claws, gouging a long scratch into Snabla's mighty shield. His eyes flashed purple, his claws elongating, glowing like otherworldly daggers.

"Hugo! Hugo, wake up! It's us!" Zelli called to him, but he was lost. Something—someone—else. Flash pounced onto Hugo's head, but was soon

ZZZZZZZZZZZZZZzzzzz

snatched up by Hugo's bearlike paws and flung away. Before she could hit the wall, she disappeared, but Zelli did not see where she reappeared. Snabla tried to deflect his blows, but the owlbear was too fearsome, too strong. Again and again Hugo's glowing claws beat against the shield, and

Snabla did his best, but he was just a young kobold and only as tall as the owlbear's knee, no match for such unrelenting strength and fury.

"My alchemy prevails!" Lord Carrion crowed. He coughed, and began to hobble away on his staff,

GRRRR!

ZZZZZZZ

putting distance between them and retreating to where the line of villagers and monsters waited.

"It's taking everything he's got to cast his spells," Bauble shrieked, tossed back and forth on Hugo's back like a rag doll. "His . . . His life force . . . He has to use his life force to hold us off! We can't give up! Magic . . . ," they wailed, almost tumbling out of the bag. "Magic 101!"

Zelli found it hard to fight when it was against her once-gentle friend. She couldn't believe it had come to this, fending off the kindest student in the entire academy, watching the kindness drain from his eyes, kindness that had led him to cook for them, and teach them, and support her even when he knew her secret. She hated to raise her sword against him, but she had to protect the others. He wasn't their friend anymore. The real Hugo was gone.

Lord Carrion's skeletons rallied, fighting alongside Hugo. "Now be torn asunder by your very own ally!"

"Bauble! Turn into something!" Zelli called. "Something, anything! Give us more than book smarts!"

The mimic tome at last tumbled free of Hugo's bag, turning a panicked circle before growing tall and thin and falling back to the ground. A skeleton

tearing toward Zelli stepped right on the shovel Bauble had become, the handle bouncing straight upward and smashing the fiend in the face. This bought Zelli time, but only a little. Not every skeleton would step on Bauble or fall for the same trick (though a surprising number did), and she soon found herself outnumbered and cornered. The wall of the cave loomed behind her, and while Snabla tried dearly to deflect Hugo's continuous onslaught, he was falling back, separated from the frozen Allidora and the trod-upon Bauble.

"Hugo!" Zelli could hear the tears rising in her voice. It hardly looked like him—she didn't recognize this cold, ferocious beast slashing at them now. Where was the kind, soft-spoken Hugo they all knew? He had to be in there somewhere. What would become of him when he finally broke free from this awful necromancer's control and realized he had harmed his own friends? She raised her sword against him, with all possible hesitation, but it was the only defense she possessed when he would not hear her desperate pleas.

There was nothing of the old, sweet Hugo left in his wild eyes.

Hugo easily batted her sword aside, and it clattered uselessly to the ground, well out of reach. When Snabla lurched forward to intercept, he,

too, was hurled away by a ferocious blow from Hugo. Zelli heard him land with a grunt somewhere in the shadows. She could see nothing now beyond Hugo—not the cave, not Allidora, not the portal Lord Carrion was undoubtedly trying again to summon. . . .

The owlbear's crushing grip landed around her upper arm and with ease, he hoisted her into the air, opening his beak wide to tear out her throat. Zelli kicked and punched but to no avail—she wasn't a real minotaur, and she didn't have a mighty owlbear's strength. She thrashed and hoped he would at least miss her neck and land somewhere less vital.

"Yes!" She heard Lord Carrion's elated shriek in the echoing vastness of the caves. "Yes! Devour her! Tear her to pieces, my thrall!"

Fitting, she thought, with a final, frightened scream—he was a monster and she a human. This was how it was always meant to end.

13

Hugo's sharpened beak came down with a snap on her shoulder joint, and she heard the crunch of bone and felt a hot splatter of blood against her chin as the owlbear took his first bite.

She expected an agonizing instant later to see her arm torn free from her body, dangling from Hugo's beak, but instead he went oddly still. His grip on her relaxed, and she heard a strangled cough from his throat before the pressure on her shoulder vanished. Hugo let go, and she slid free and alive to the floor. The owlbear, still with strange and possessed eyes, spat, pawing listlessly at his own tongue.

Even under the necromancer's control, Hugo's distaste for flesh could not be undone.

The distraction gave Snabla the chance to whack his shield down hard on Hugo's foot, while

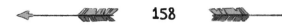

Zelli searched the shattered skeletal bones littering the cave floor until she found a shard sharp enough to serve as a knife. Hugo noticed her and raised his arm to swing, but not before she dove under his armpit and slashed the purple, tainted fur and feathers near his elbow. The ooze congealed on the floor, waiting for another unsuspecting victim to snare. At once, his eyes went dim, then bright again, and he raised his hands to find the blood staining his claws, wailing.

"What . . . What have I done?"

"Nothing that a bone setter can't fix," Zelli replied, laughing with short-lived relief. Her left shoulder was badly wounded, and she could hardly lift that arm. With her right hand, she took the help Hugo offered, and stood at his side once more.

"Are you . . . Did I . . ."

"*You* didn't do anything; the necromancer controlled you with that magical goop. We can worry about that later, just be grateful you only like vegetables," Zelli told him, hurrying back toward the frozen Allidora and Bauble, who had now drawn the attention of too many skeletons. One swept up Bauble, holding the shovel high, preparing to snap them in half. The mimic transformed just in time, into a heavy iron-bound treasure chest, crushing

crack

CRUNCH

crack

the skeleton under their weight.

Injured, Zelli let Hugo hoist her onto his shoulders while he and Snabla led the way as they returned to Bauble, the last few skeletons swarming. She felt strange and jittery without her training sword, but she had lost it in the fight, not that she could wield it anyway with her severely injured arm. Hugo, now enraged in his own right, bashed them with his heavy fists, just as any owlbear might do, but *their* owlbear this time. Minion after minion flew across the cave, crumbling as their frail bodies hit the stone. Flash couldn't help herself, popping up just in time to catch a broken leg bone before it could reach the floor. While Hugo charged, Flash happily munched her bone, tail wagging. Zelli pretended it was her way of cheering them on. That thought lasted only an instant, as Flash promptly disappeared again with her bone.

At last, Lord Carrion noticed his control over Hugo had waned, and he began muttering his spell faster and faster, sliding down the staff propping him up, the portal just the suggestion of a purple oval, weak and translucent. As his magic failed and so did his stamina, the barrier holding Allidora dissipated, letting her tumble forward a few steps before glancing around in confusion, chest heaving.

"After him!" Zelli cried, and even grievously injured, even in terrible pain, she found the power to let loose a resounding roar. The others were with her now—Snabla with his shield proudly raised; Bauble's treasure chest flying forward like a battering ram; Hugo wielding his claws like knives; Allidora Steelstrike readying her broadsword with her azure cape flying about her shoulders.

The necromancer sneered, alone, with no more bones to raise and protect him. He did not yield but looked instead to the line of villagers and monsters obediently waiting. . . .

"Do not let him use that army against us! They are innocents!" Allidora called.

Ahead, appearing out of thin air, Flash landed right on top of Lord Carrion's pointy head, the bone snack trailing from her snout knocking his hood back. The necromancer flailed,

stumbling, looking, in that moment, not like a wizard of great power but like an enfeebled craven stumbling into defeat. The heroes were upon him, and Allidora didn't need to use her sword, and Hugo didn't need to flash his claws—Snabla slammed right into his legs, sending the necromancer end over end and into a dusty, musty corner. They gathered around him, triumphant and exhausted, catching their breath while the necromancer cowered at their feet.

"Children! You can delay me, but you cannot delay the inevitable. More will come; more will come in service of my lord. Their souls will be ours, the engine will be powered," he wheezed, his staff knocked aside. He reached for it with trembling hands, but it was too late. Bauble drew near to him, and the necromancer spat. "What will you become, you useless creature? Nothing that can bring you power over one such as—"

But Bauble had heard enough; they all had. The mimic changed rapidly into an iron pan, and Zelli had the strength left in her right arm to grab them just in time, wind up, and swing with all her might and will, knocking the necromancer out of his wits before he could finish his vile spew. With no sword to swing, the pan just had to do.

"Not so useless after all," Bauble laughed,

transforming from the heavy pan back to an even heavier book.

Allidora Steelstrike strode to the necromancer and fished a bit of rope from her belt, tying his hands and taking his staff, cracking it in two over her knee and scattering the pieces. A shock wave rippled out from the broken weapon, a shimmering, cascading tide that swept across the cave, nearly knocking the villagers and monsters to the ground. At once, the spell cast over the villagers began to fade, dozens and dozens of blinking, shocked eyes peering at them as the ensorcelled folk found themselves not at home in bed or sitting at the hearth, but deep in a cold and forgotten cave.

"Be calm!" Allidora said, at once taking control of the situation. She sheathed her sword on her back and raised her arms, calming the sudden outcry from the lost and confounded victims. "All is not well, but all will be well—"

"Some of them are monsters," Zelli whispered at her side. "I don't want them harmed." And here she pointed to a bugbear visible among the snaking line of villagers. The woman beside the monster let out a shriek, backing away and into the arms of a human man, perhaps her husband, who held her and shielded her from the student.

Allidora raised a dark brow but then gave a single, precise nod. "Hmm. I see." Then she addressed the murmuring crowd again. "Your questions will be answered in time, but not here. This cave is not safe for us to linger; return the way you came, and with as much haste as you can muster." She must have noticed the spider eggs and chittering, too. "There are some among you that may seem like enemies . . ." Her gaze swiftly roamed the line of anxious, fidgeting villagers. "Bugbear and goblin, and here owlbear and kobold, but do them no harm; they, too, were fooled by the necromancer's spell. They even fought beside me, if for just a time. Behold: Lord Carrion, our shared enemy. His fell magic is to blame for this mayhem, and he will

be dealt with accordingly. Now, return peacefully to the clearing above, and there I will escort you back to Horntree Village."

"That's Allidora Steelstrike," she heard one of the men in the crowd whisper. "We best do as she says...."

"She's a hero, is she not?" another whispered.

So on and so on the message traveled up the line. The halfling girl at the front was steered around by the woman behind her, and gradually the befuddled masses shuffled back up the long, narrow stone bridge that had brought them so close to doom. Zelli couldn't help but wonder how many had actually gone through the portal before they could stop Lord Carrion, and where they might have gone. She shuddered, terrified for them. She also couldn't help but be grateful for Allidora's presence—she couldn't imagine how the folk might have responded to just her and her classmates after Lord Carrion was defeated.

"You're wounded," the adventurer said, turning to Zelli. "Here, walk with me. The walk back to the cave mouth will allow us time to talk."

Allidora deftly bandaged Zelli's shoulder with a piece of cloth torn from her bright blue cape, while Hugo hoisted the bound and unconscious necromancer over his shoulder. Her friends started the

trek up to the cave mouth first, only Snabla shooting a curious gaze back, his eyes going wide as he finally realized the resemblance.

"Oh," he muttered. "Oh!"

Hugo nudged him with a foot, and they gave the two humans a measure of privacy. The tangle of questions and feelings and fears knotting up in Zelli's stomach almost made her forget the throb in her shoulder. She clutched her wound, hissing through her teeth.

"I must confess, I did not expect to be helped by such . . . such an unlikely party," Allidora said, smirking. It was Zelli's smirk, and it stole her breath away to see it so plainly. "Those monsters he magicked, you know them?"

"Of them," Zelli replied. Her tongue felt impossibly thick and clumsy in her mouth. "They're some of the older, popular kids, so they don't really give us the time of day. But when we came to save them, we didn't expect to find, well, all of this trouble."

They were quiet for a moment, then Allidora made a soft, thoughtful sound in her throat. Zelli knew what was coming, that they both knew, that the obvious features they shared were too much for anyone with even rudimentary observation skills not to note. Even Snabla had put it all together. It

was easier to just talk of what had happened, and Zelli almost hoped they could do that forever, and never touch the raw, painful wound waiting there between them.

But then, of course, Allidora spoke again, and the tangle in Zelli's stomach grew tighter and crueler and even more impossible. "And when you struck out to find them, when you came to this place, did you expect then to find your mother, Zellidora?"

14

Zelli clutched her wounded shoulder with her right hand, her heart drumming and drumming against her wrist, her pulse a wild and reckless fluttering that robbed her of breath and thought. Though the injury throbbed, Allidora Steelstrike had bound the wound expertly, and despite the difficult pain, Zelli felt confident it would heal in time. Less certain to heal were the gaping wounds that remained bloodied and raw from her past, and now, trudging up the stone bridge with her mother, in her present.

"I didn't know what I would find," Zelli replied. She reached back and plucked off the fake minotaur tail swinging from her trousers, and shoved it into her trouser pocket. It was foolish to keep wearing it, to pretend. "There were . . . rumors. Rumors a Steelstrike might be near the village.

 171

So I risked it. I found your illustration in a book about—" She caught herself. "Heroes. We look so much alike, I thought we had to be related. So, I listened to those rumors, and now here I am."

"Oh, Zellidora," the woman said, pausing and reaching over to take the girl's hand. She expected to feel something right away, a jolt, a reminder of their shared blood, but it was just another hand touching hers. "I'm glad you did."

"Nobody calls me Zellidora," she muttered, turned, and kept walking. Still, she couldn't help but glance now and then at the woman who was her mother. Was this what she would look like in time? Refined and honed, with scars crisscrossing her face and forearms, with broad shoulders and sturdy limbs? "I go by Zelli."

"Zelli." Allidora tested out the name. "Ha. When I was your age, I did the same, hated

my name. Insisted everyone from the baker to my swordmaster call me Alli."

That doesn't mean anything. That doesn't mean we're the same.

Zelli shrugged, then winced from the pain of it. "I thought I would have questions. Now I don't even know where to start."

"I do." Allidora sighed and shook her head, thick curls bouncing on her nape. The temperature warmed as they climbed back toward the surface, the occasional torch spitting and hissing as they passed. The topmost level of the cave was still not in sight. They still had time. Zelli washed her hands over each other. "I owe you so much, but I'll start with an apology. And an explanation."

"I don't need—" It just came out. Why try to stop her? That was why she had come, why she had risked her life and the lives of the others. . . . But now it was too close, too real, and the thought that the truth might hurt too much hadn't occurred to her until then. Anything was better than thinking her family had abandoned her for stupid reasons.

"You *do* need to know," Allidora interrupted. She grunted and rolled her shoulders, her neck popping as loud as a twig snapped in the dead of night. "I am sure you won't believe me, Zellidora—Zelli, apologies—but I put you in the basket that

day because I loved you more than anything. But more than that, because of that, I wanted you to survive. I am so sorry for what I did, but not for loving you enough to try and spare you my sort of life."

They shuffled by another torch bolted to a drooping stalactite, and with the warm light bathing them both, Allidora lifted her right hand, twisting it back and forth. One of her fingers was slightly shorter than it ought to be, and what flesh was visible beneath a furred vambrace was mottled with heavy scars. "I watched my parents ride off one day to deal with a wounded dragon just south of Baldur's Gate. My father sat me down at a table by the hearth and lit a tall candle. He kissed me on both cheeks and told me they would be back even before that candle burned down." She pressed her lips together and glanced sidelong at Zelli. "Well, that candle burned down. And another, too. And another. The fire went out and the house was cold, and my parents never returned. Steelstrikes never get to choose the adventuring life; we're handed a sword before we can even heft it. The rest is hard, and bloody, and over before it's even really begun."

Venting a dry laugh, she gingerly brushed the bandage on Zelli's shoulder. "I was hoping a nice

farming family would find you, or maybe you'd be a bookseller's daughter, that you'd be spared all of this, that you'd never have to watch the candles burn down while your heart turned to ash. But I suppose it's in the blood. Adventuring found you, try as I might." She paused and looked away, her brow furrowing. "I did look for you, you know. I thought it would put my heart at ease if I knew a kind family had found you, but no matter who I asked, or what letters I wrote, nobody could say where you had gone. It . . . troubled me greatly to think harm had befallen you, daughter."

Zelli paused at the next wider landing, the snaking trail of villagers and monsters leaving them behind in the quieting gloom. "You wanted me?"

"Yes, I wanted you. *We* wanted you. Your father is gone now, too, felled by a white dragon three winters past. Wanting you was not enough— the greater urge was to protect you, to see that you did not become another fallen adventurer. Giving you a chance at life, that was the better path, I thought. The kindest path. It left me with less, but you with more." Allidora looked beyond her daughter, toward Hugo, Snabla, Bauble, and Flash. "But whatever fate I left you to . . . What have I done? These monsters . . . These are your kin now?"

Zelli didn't appreciate her tone and showed as much by grimacing and leaving her behind, walking swiftly up the next curved stone bridge leading toward the cave mouth. No more eggs or webs. They were almost free of this accursed place.

"I meant no offense," her mother said, catching up to her easily.

"But you gave it." Zelli sliced her hand through the air, hot and stinging tears gathering in her eyes. "Without us you wouldn't have defeated Lord Carrion, remember? They are my friends. *They* are reliable. Hugo is gentle and kind, and never has a cross word for anyone. Bauble might be a mimic, but they're so, so smart. And Snabla? He charged into the fire with a wooden shield; he didn't know it was magic. He was ready to die for all of us. If that isn't bravery, then what is? They're not just monsters. You could learn something from them."

Allidora hung her head, and it didn't suit her. It was hard to imagine the bold warrior looking anything but brave and confident. "I see. I'm sure I deserved that." But the wind had gone out of her. Perking up, she watched Zelli from behind a curl fallen free, swinging in front of her forehead. "You don't need to tell me your story, or what happened,

or how you've fared these eleven years—that might not be mine to know—but you might tell me one thing. . . ."

"One thing," Zelli repeated. She supposed she could give her one. "Like what?"

"Do you prefer that life?" Allidora Steelstrike asked, keeping her distance now. They had reached the brighter landing just before the cave entrance. Scattered bones from Lord Carrion's fallen servants littered the floor, magenta dawn light spilling onto the stones. "Do you truly feel like you belong? Like they are your home? But how could that be? A Steelstrike living among . . . It just doesn't seem right."

Outside, Hugo, Snabla, Bauble, and Flash waited for her. Hugo bounced listlessly from foot to foot, shooting nervous glances into the cave, checking on her. Did she belong with them, or with the woman—the human—waiting patiently for her answer?

"No part of this seems right. I thought meeting you, or anyone from my family, would make everything fall into place, that I would know right away I was meant to be with you, and I could leave this other life behind, that in the end it would all be easier," Zelli sighed. "None of this is easier. None of it makes any sense."

"You could come with me. Now that I know there is no keeping you from the sword, I might as well train you myself." She took up her blade, showing its fine craftsmanship, its sharpness and weight to Zelli. "At least if I'm by your side, I know

you're protected. Come, Zellidora. You're a Steel-strike. This life, these blades, these glories, they are your birthright."

"Zelli?"

Hugo had called softly, experimentally, into the cave. From their vantage, they probably couldn't see much of anything. They were waiting for her, and she felt her heels itch, and unexpectedly she knew her answer.

Finding the emblem pin tucked into her belt, Zelli held it in her hand and then rubbed her thumb over the engraving thoughtfully. Allidora stared down at the symbol, then smiled and nodded. Her birthright. But the metal felt cold in her hand, and hollow, more like a child's dress-up brooch than anything she wanted to inherit. She held out the badge to her mother.

"You can have this back. I already have some-one to train me and protect me. She's been doing it all my life."

Allidora frowned, then sighed, folding Zelli's fingers back over the badge, forcing her to hold on to it. "Keep it; you might need it one day. These Steelstrike emblems are not mere decoration; they are enchanted with powerful magic. They call to each other. Everyone in our clan carries one, and should you need me, simply hold the emblem tight

and speak the words, 'By sword and by light, Talos guide my sight, summon my kin, call the Steelstrike.' Can you remember that?"

Zelli repeated the words silently in her head and nodded.

"The emblem will become a beacon for me to find you, and if you speak those words, I will come. May I ask . . . The folk who found you . . . Who—what—are they?"

Zelli closed her eyes tightly. "I don't think you want to know that. Your entire life is hunting monsters, hunting the kind of creatures who gave me a family. All you need to know is that they love me." Her chin dipped, and she felt the rush of tears come on again. This time she let the tears go, and realized she wasn't crying for Allidora or the life she lost with her, but for the mothers she had callously run from. "They love me and I . . . I abandoned them. Just like you abandoned me."

Allidora slumped and looked to the side, then righted herself and placed a solid hand on Zelli's good shoulder. "If they love you, if they are your true family, then they will forgive you. I would. Why you left matters. Listen, I . . . I won't ask that you forgive me, Zelli, but are you certain? Are you sure this is what you want?"

"No," Zelli said. "But it's my answer."

"Then keep that," Allidora replied, suddenly lurching forward and pulling Zelli into her arms. She held her for a moment, and Zelli froze, but let her take that time. When Allidora pulled back, she didn't spare her another glance, but rushed headlong out of the cave, her voice just above a whisper. "You could change your mind, and when you do, I'll be waiting."

15

ow with the benefit of the brightening sky, Zelli could see clearly the churned dirt overlook just outside the cave. To the west, waves crashed far below on jagged rocks, and to the east, the forest spread out tall and intimidating, the solitary trees at the very edge standing like sharpened pikes guarding a dark and sleepy town. A path carved its way through those woods, its mud splattered with purple ooze and covered in tracks. The villagers huddled there, just off the path, all of them avoiding the remains of the alchemy that had put them under the necromancer's control.

And of course, south and south again lay just the vaguest imprint of the dull and uninteresting mountain they called home. She hadn't expected to go so far and then yearn for it, for the same old, but she did.

Allidora Steelstrike inspected each of her companions with a wry, lifted brow, watching as Hugo swept Zelli into a tight embrace, then remembered her arm and set her down gently. "Oh! Forgive me, forgive me!" Hugo cried. Snabla raised his shield in salute to Zelli, while Flash popped out of Hugo's bag to give the girl a big, long lick on the cheek before returning to the safety of the backpack.

After seeing all of this, Allidora hitched her baldric higher and gave Zelli a nod. What that nod meant, Zelli would ponder for a long time.

"I'm taking a jar of this stuff back to my guild,"

Steelstrike said. "Carrion wasn't the first necromancer spotted in this region, and he won't be the last. Whomever he serves will come looking for him soon." She shook her head and began wandering toward the villagers, preparing to be their guide for the journey back to their charred homes. Roofs could be mended and walls remade, but the absence of those who went through the portal would be felt until they were found, if ever. "Somehow, Zellidora, I don't think this will be the last time we meet."

"Zelli," she corrected her, standing close to her friends. She took out the little tail she had worn in her school days, crumpled but intact, and tucked it into the back of her trousers.

Steelstrike snorted softly. "Right."

When the woman was a safe distance away, Snabla whipped his head around and glared up at Zelli. "Human go with human. Why ssstill here?"

"I don't know," she said, half meaning it. "Zelli Stormclash just has a better ring to it."

Hugo's beak split into a grin, his head cocking to the side and his feathers ruffing around his neck. "You traversed the maze," said the owlbear. "And found the minotaur."

Rolling her eyes, Zelli dragged her exhausted body back toward the cave, kneeling to inspect

the wet purple ooze gathered on the skeleton they had defeated there. "That is *so* corny."

But she didn't say it wasn't true.

"We should take our own glob of that," Bauble piped up from Hugo's bag, tucked there again with their now steady companion, Flash. The blink dog had tired herself out with all the antics and skeleton slaying, and dozed softly, whiskers fluttering with each soft and rumbling snore. "The academy professors will want to study it."

"Where are the others?" Zelli asked, standing and squinting into the horizon as it split open, the golden light there widening, casting a gleaming haze across the overlook.

"There!" Hugo pointed down the coastline. The villagers had already filtered back into the woods, led away by Allidora Steelstrike.

Zelli caught one last glimpse of her cape before the adventurer—the Horrible Human in the flesh—was gone.

As Zelli peered into the sunrise, a round, blobular form sharpened into the silhouette of Dean Zxaticus, the beholder floating along the coast toward them. Their lost and found classmates Patty and Gutrash were with him, as well as Professor Cantrip, caught in his gelatinous cube, as well as a rather ornate carriage, which Zelli quickly realized was the mimic professor Impro Vice.

The bugbear and goblin appeared dazed, gazing up at the professors with what Zelli could only consider a lost puppy expression.

"Professors!" Bauble exclaimed, bouncing along on Hugo's back as they all hurried to meet the adults down the coast.

Round, immense, quivering with tentacles, Dean Zxaticus's one cunning eye inspected them all from top to bottom. His gaze lingered on Zelli, hornless, her tail tacked on but askew, and her shoulder quite obviously bleeding through a makeshift bandage.

"It appears we were not the first to launch an investigation," Professor Cantrip burbled from inside the green ooze. "Kifin Stormclash's concerns were well-founded."

"Indeed," the dean boomed. They quavered under his sight and his scolding tone. Hugo in particular appeared ready to bolt for the woods in fright. But the beholder's voice softened, his spherical body swishing side to side as if shaking his head. "By all the gods and oaths, what were you four thinking?"

His attention traveled back to Zelli, but she froze.

"But we saved them!" Bauble blurted out, only just visible over Hugo's shoulder. "We only wanted to save our classmates." Their voice dwindled to a squeak. "We're . . . We're heroes."

"Heroes, indeed!" cried Impro Vice, angry eyes

now glaring at them from the carriage front box. "Bauble Ephemera Tchotchke the Forty-Seventh, when your spawn parent hears of this—"

"But it'sss true," rasped Gutrash the goblin, glancing nervously from professor to professor. "When I could think again with my own mind, I saw them there, ssstanding victoriousss over the necromancer." He pointed to the slumped and limp form of Lord Carrion, who Hugo had unceremoniously deposited next to the cave mouth. "It wasss them!"

If the testimonies of Patty and Gutrash weren't sufficient, then the state of Lord Carrion ought to be proof enough of their involvement. Before leaving him for the professors to deal with, Snabla had insisted on using a bit of Hugo's pack strap to tie a sign around the necromancer's neck that read simply, STINKY.

Bauble had begrudgingly helped with the spelling.

"They vanquished him," Patty added, shier than Gutrash, apparently cowed by the commanding presence of the beholder. "They did it with the human adventurer!"

She then stared deliberately at Zelli's hornless head, the truth of her human nature dawning on the bugbear, albeit slowly. At that, Zelli stepped surreptitiously behind Hugo, hiding.

"Hmm. Most interesting. *Most* interesting. However this feat was accomplished, we owe these students our respect." His tone shifted, more pointed, sterner, and he seemed to direct this to Patty and Gutrash most of all. "I expect there will be no specific discussion of how the necromancer was defeated once we return to the campus, and furthermore, I will require you all to meet with our counselor, Nihildris, after this most troubling event."

Gutrash groaned and rolled his eyes, but Patty elbowed him hard in the stomach. Nobody wanted to get called to the counselor's office. Nihildris, the mind flayer, would twirl his eerie tentacles

around his fingers and brood, and never dispense guidance so much as burn guidance directly into the brain. Zelli couldn't help but worry that Patty and Gutrash wouldn't listen to the principal *or* the counselor, and that her secret, her *human* secret, would soon be an open one. She always suspected the staff knew, on some level, and that they said nothing as a favor to Kifin. Zelli's status as the sole minotaur on campus had allowed her to remain mysterious and strange, but now she would be the center of attention.

At last, the beholder's attention switched to the unconscious necromancer behind them. "It seems I have much to discuss with the staff, and much to discern. We will collect this necromancer and return to the academy so that he may be . . . *questioned.*"

"The adventurer seemed convinced of more necromancers in the area," said Bauble, finding their voice again. "Some of the students went through a portal he conjured, but we don't know where he intended to take them."

"He spoke of a m-master," stammered Hugo.

"Ssstinky master," agreed Snabla. "A lord building an army of soulsss, coming to take all the villagers and ssstudents!"

"Students? Grave." Dean Zxaticus went rigid,

and Zelli noticed the other professors did, too. Were they afraid? "Most grave. We have much to do if we are to locate these abducted students." Then he paused, and said very clearly, "We, as in your professors. There will be no more heroics from the four of you. And do not consider your success immunity from punishment," the dean growled. "There will be consequences for breaking curfew and leaving school grounds, even if your intentions were noble."

He fixed his one big eye and all his many tentacled eyestalks on Zelli again, and she knew their conversation was far from over. She could only imagine what they all must have thought when their absence was clear and her goodbye note discovered. Facing the dean, she thought, wasn't half so terrifying as facing her mothers.

The dean then floated away to inspect the necromancer, while Professor Cantrip took Patty and Gutrash aside to question them. Impro Vice followed the dean, no doubt prepared to be the method of conveyance for their captive.

"Ssstupid grown-upsss, why trouble for usss? We help! We sssave!" Snabla kicked at the dirt with his little clawed feet.

"I think we're just lucky we're not expelled," Zelli sighed. She rubbed at her eyes with one hand

and yawned. They were each of them covered in mud, muck, and pulverized bone, clothes torn and knees scraped. "I hope Zxaticus can teleport us back. I don't think I can walk one more step."

"And you are sure about all of this?" Hugo asked, beaming down at her. "None of us would think less of you if you wanted to go and join your kind."

"Sssnabla would think less!" the kobold shrieked.

"Yes," she chuckled, watching Snabla thrust his arms crossly over his chest. "I'm sure. Besides, you're my adventuring party now, right? And you never split the party."

16

"I can explain," Zelli murmured. It was the only thing she could think of to say now that she faced two bewildered minotaurs. Bewilderment became shock and then relief, and in the next moment, Zelli was scooped up by two pairs of very strong, very furry arms.

The dean had indeed taken pity on the students and teleported them back to the academy, sparing them all the exhausting journey. Still covered in mud and smelling wretched, bleeding, tired, and dragging her bag behind her, Zelli made her way to the modest chambers allotted to her mother as a staff member at the school. Even just the short trudge from the dean's office to their home left her feeling further bedraggled and raw, and when she nudged open the tall, gnarled wooden door, the familiar sights and smells almost made her fall

down right then and there. The sitting room rug looked plenty inviting for a well-earned nap.

But instead, her mothers rushed to find her and embrace her, and the moment they swept her up, Zelli knew she had made the right choice.

"You do not need to explain anything," Professor Stormclash told her, letting her down to the ground but not releasing her tight grip on Zelli. "We always worried. . . . And we always knew you would wonder, too."

"But you're back," Iasme said, clasping her hands together and kneeling. Then she reached out and fondly pushed her hand through Zelli's hair. "You came back to us; that's all that matters."

"B-But I'm sorry," Zelli blubbered. Maybe it wasn't until that moment, at last indisputably, perfectly safe and sound, that she realized how

close she had come to real harm. Many skilled, seasoned adventurers ran afoul of necromancers and paid with their lives. She went boneless and sagged to the floor, and felt the comforting touch of the rug beneath her fingers, something so small and simple but so reassuring.

Home.

"I belong here," she said softly, sitting back on her heels and dredging up a smile. "This is home."

"Home, yes," Professor Stormclash repeated, matching her daughter's smile, maybe not perfectly, but in the way a minotaur could. "Home with your family."

There was so much Zelli wanted to say but didn't. Couldn't. Maybe one day it would all tumble out, or after she had been able to sort it into neat piles, she could explain the rush of confusion and emotions she had felt meeting and fighting alongside her birth mother. But it wasn't time, not yet. How could she say it all and not sound mad, or worse, ungrateful?

I met my mother, but it didn't feel the same. There was nothing there but a face like mine and a voice like mine; there wasn't any love or recognition or memory. I wasn't hers and she wasn't mine. And I missed all of this—the little hearth with its smoky chimney, the ugly crocheted blankets Iasme

 195

made, the old academy pennants from their days at the school, the mismatched chairs, one just a bit taller so I can reach the table....

"I'm sorry I ruined your birthday," she said instead.

"You're here with us again." Carefully, Professor Stormclash lifted Zelli's chin and shook out her mane, sighing. "That is gift enough. Nothing is ruined now that you are safe."

"Oh, but she isn't!" Iasme gasped, at last noticing the torn bandage looped around Zelli's shoulder. Climbing to her feet, the minotaur thundered away to the kitchen, cupboards opening and closing with a crash as she rummaged and muttered to herself.

"We defeated a necromancer," Zelli told her, the magnitude of it still a strange thing to carry. But her mother didn't express an instant of surprise and took it all in stride.

"Of course you did, Zelli—you're the pride of the Stormclash minotaurs."

And then the wound of course took precedence, and the expected fussing began, but that was all right with her. Even that, Zelli thought, which usually annoyed her to no end, was something good, something she would have dearly missed.

Home, she thought. *Now I can rest.*

Back in the dining chamber, nothing much had changed. The goblins ate with the goblins, the oozes slorped with the oozes, and the myconids multiplied with the other myconids. On that day or any other, though that day in particular, a snapping cold winter afternoon just before semester break, Zelli found herself wedged at the end of a half-broken table, horns on her head, tail pinned to her trousers, listening to Snabla retell—yet again—the legend of their great victory over the necromancer.

"Then Zelli Ssstormclash took the pan and sssmashed it over his head!"

With Snabla's underbite and peculiar arrangement of teeth, "Stormclash" was a particularly challenging word for him. None of them commented, but just calmly wiped the spittle off their lunches while the kobold hurried on.

Zelli smiled to herself, somewhere else, the thought of the cave and the skeletal army and the necromancer's voice making her heart race only a little bit. The nightmares had been terrible for a while, and she had slept sandwiched between her two minotaur mothers until she could manage the night on her own and returned to her dormitory room on steadier feet. She reached into her belt, feeling the Steelstrike badge she always kept

pinned there, hidden but not forgotten.

It felt like a dream, meeting Allidora, looking, for the first time, into the face of another human. She had expected to feel so much, and for everything to be clear. Weeks on, nothing was clear, but she didn't feel the specter of regret looming, either, so she decided that was a win.

"You're telling it all wrong," Bauble grumbled. They were about to correct Snabla's every minor mistake in the retelling when Gutrash walked by their table, haunch of meat in hand, his eyes drifting to them quickly and then darting away. Zelli saw him give the faintest nod of acknowledgment, all they could expect even after saving the day.

She wondered if he and Patty had rewritten it all in their heads. Sometimes Zelli caught herself doing the same—she gave herself fluctuating amounts of credit, sometimes thinking she had defeated a dozen skeletons, other times twenty. Maybe Patty and Gutrash didn't want to admit that a bunch of dumb kids had won the day, and that they had allied with a vile human adventurer to do it. Maybe it was easier to just let life go on as it always did.

But it couldn't. Zelli felt a big elbow nudge her and met Hugo's gaze. She knew he was thinking the same thing—those other students were out

there somewhere. Lost.

"The professors will find them," Hugo murmured, far quieter than Snabla's regaling.

"I know," Zelli said, but she didn't. What she didn't tell him, couldn't yet tell him, was that she had overheard her mothers discussing the missing students. Zxaticus wanted to enlist the help of

Zelli, Bauble, Hugo, and Snabla in locating those who had vanished through the portal. They were the only ones to have fought and defeated the necromancer, so their help might prove useful. Iasme and Kifin were, unsurprisingly, not thrilled about this development.

Everyone was so pleased with themselves, so proud, it didn't seem right to bring down the mood. Besides, there would be plenty of time to tell them the news. And maybe Zxaticus would change his mind. She couldn't decide if she wanted him to or not.

"Hey!" Bauble suddenly interrupted, loud enough to startle Flash, who had taken to slumbering peacefully in Hugo's massive book bag. The blink dog came tumbling out, spilling Zelli's milk. It was only a momentary mess, as Flash immediately set about licking up the puddle. Four tomes, miscellaneous sprigs of herbs, a troubling number of mushrooms, dirt, and a bundle of carrots could be seen inside the bag as well before Hugo latched it shut sheepishly and hid it next to his chair.

"Thisss better be important!" Snabla snapped at them.   slurp
                                                                     slurp
Zelli scooped up
Flash and let the

pup sit contentedly in her lap, asleep even before Bauble said their next words.

"We never chose a name for ourselves," said Bauble, themselves appearing as a book, and also sitting on a stack of books so they could be tall enough to see over the table with the others. "If we're a real adventuring party, then we need a name."

Snabla rolled his beady eyes. "Not thisss again."

"You know we'll never agree on anything," Zelli reminded them.

"Sssnabla's Snakes!" the kobold cried, banging his fist on the table, nearly spilling Zelli's milk again. "All for Sssnabla and Snabla for All! Kobold Crushersss! Ssservants of Snabla!"

"Oh!" Hugo grinned, and mildly tucked his hands together on the table, feathers ruffled with excitement. He had already devoured his salad, leaving nothing but a single tiny mushroom cap on the plate. "I have an idea."

"It will be ssstupid, but say," replied Snabla, pouting.

"Let's hear it, then," Bauble encouraged him.

Zelli said nothing, but let go of the badge inside her belt, giving Hugo her full and undivided attention. She was glad that he had finally stopped sending long-winded, flowery apology notes to

her dormitory, page after page of his abject horror at having almost bitten her arm off. The first time it was kind of nice, but by the fifth letter, her roommate was beginning to get the wrong impression.

"Go on," Zelli told him. "What should we call ourselves?"

"Perhaps I should begin with a brief introduction and methodology behind my suggestion. You see, it all began in 1220 DR when the dark prince—"

"Ssspit it out!"

"Very well." Hugo's feathers puffed further, but then he drew in a deep breath and spread his clawed hands wide. "Danger Club."

"Danger Club," Zelli repeated, trying it on the tongue. "All right. I like that, it fits."

Bauble's scrollwork mouth quirked to the side. "I approve, but Snabla will never agree to it."

"Ha! Shows what dummy dum-dum mimic knowsss. Snabla like!"

"Then it's settled," Bauble chirped, their appearance changing ever so slightly, and as they all observed, the gilded letters reshaped across their cover until the title read, in curlicue fantastical text, *The Most Daring Legends and Deeds of the Danger Club.*

"Deeds," Hugo read, pulling his head back in

surprise. "But we have performed but one deed. Does this mean we are not finished?"

Zelli picked up her porridge spoon and grinned down into her food. "Finished? We still have our classmates to find. We are not finished, Hugo. We're a long, long way from graduation. We're only getting started."